THE AMISH BACHELOR

SEVEN AMISH BACHELORS BOOK 1

SAMANTHA PRICE

AMISH ROMANCE

Copyright © 2017 Samantha Price

All rights reserved.

No part of this book may be reproduced in any form or by any electronic or mechanical means, including information storage and retrieval systems, without written permission from the author, except for the use of brief quotations in a book review.

Scripture quotations from The Authorized (King James) Version. Rights in the Authorized Version in the United Kingdom are vested in the Crown. Reproduced by permission of the Crown's patentee, Cambridge University Press.

This is a work of fiction. Any names or characters, businesses or places, events or incidents, are fictitious. Any resemblance to actual persons, living or dead, or actual events is purely coincidental.

CHAPTER 1

Isaac Fuller breathed in the fresh air as his horse pulled the buggy toward his family's kitchen joinery workshop. Even though his six brothers and his father all worked various jobs within the company, Isaac was first to arrive at work every morning and that was just the way he liked it.

With his father gradually doing less, Isaac had stepped up to take over many of his areas of expertise. With permission from their Amish bishop, in addition to having electricity in their workshop, they were allowed computers. Like the bishops in most of the communities these days, theirs knew the hardships of keeping up with competitors without use of a website or offering online ordering facilities. Isaac had overseen the development of their website two years ago and that had moved the business along greatly. Now

Isaac had worked through putting all their accounts and invoices onto the accounting system on the computer. That had been a mammoth task, but now that it was done, it made things like the monthly bookkeeping a lot easier.

There was nothing Isaac liked better than opening the doors of the workshop, flicking on the coffee machine, filling his mug, and then scrolling through the new emails while sipping his morning coffee. Before his rowdy brothers arrived, yes, that was his best time of day.

When he put the key into the lock, the door opened without him turning the key. His heart beat fast. His first thought was that they'd been robbed. As he took a step inside, he saw that the lights were on.

"Hello?" he yelled out. He'd warned his father not to keep cash on the premises, but as with most things, his father had dug his heels in and still refused to make daily visits to the bank. Thankfully, most of their transactions these days were by credit card or direct deposit.

"Jah?" came a small female voice.

He stepped in further, his heart rate calming a bit. "Who's there?"

"It's Hazel Bauer."

He followed the voice to his office and saw her sitting on his chair behind his desk at his computer. "Can I help you?"

"Nee, I'm fine." She stood up and the chair screeched

along the floor. She reached out her hand. "I'm Hazel Bauer."

He shook her hand. "And what are you doing here?"

"I'm doing the bookwork. You must be one of the Fuller boys."

"Jah, I'm Isaac." He realized this must've been his father's doing. "How did you get in?"

"Your *vadder* gave me a key. I like to start early and he said no one gets here before eight."

Isaac pressed his lips together tightly. He always got there before seven, and his father knew that. He stared at the girl. She was now sitting again, looking at the screen while tapping a calculator. She was fair-skinned with a pleasant face and unusual large green eyes.

Those eyes! He moved closer to get a better look at her. Could she be that same girl? She looked the same, but older. "Where are you from?"

"I'm from a small community near Allentown."

She couldn't be one and the same, he thought, since she gave no sign that she recognized him. If he didn't already have a girlfriend he might have been pleased to have a girl such as her in the workplace. But seeing her sitting in his seat and doing his job, he wasn't so happy. "So, what's the story? My *vadder* has employed you, or what?"

She stopped and looked up at him. "Oh, didn't he tell you?"

He shook his head.

"Jah, I'm working here full-time now, doing the bookwork and all the accounting. I've been fully trained in it. I had my last job for two years and they were very happy with my work."

He folded his arms across his chest. "Why did you leave?"

She looked away from him. "I ... I wanted to move here."

"You've moved here recently?"

"I have, just yesterday."

"With your husband?"

She giggled. *"Nee,* just myself."

It was odd for a single girl to move to a different community without an apparent good reason, such as moving there for a man. Young Amish women just didn't move by themselves for nothing. "Don't you have a family?"

"I do, but not here." She turned back to her computer and kept working.

The coffee was calling him. He'd talk to his father later in the day and find out what was going on. Wasn't his father happy with the job he'd been doing? Why did he have to call someone else in? And tell him nothing about it? He turned to leave, and then turned back around. "I usually check the emails every morning at this computer."

She pointed to the office next to hers, which was his

father's. "There's another one in there—a computer, I mean."

He did his best to hide his annoyance. She didn't even stop working to speak with him; every time there had been a lull in the conversation she went right back to working. "If you have trouble figuring out the system, or if you need any help, let me know."

He went to walk away, and she said, "The last woman who did the accounting for you made a few errors, but it's nothing I can't fix."

His mouth fell open. "Errors?" *Woman? What makes her think only women do bookwork?* he wondered.

"*Jah,* she made some little mistakes. I don't think she fully knew how the software worked. It won't take me long to fix, hopefully." She glanced up at him and smiled before she began tapping the keys again.

He walked away, heading to the lunchroom. He'd put all the new systems in, and to hear that he'd made mistakes didn't make him happy. But had he made mistakes, or was that her way of justifying her job there? He was too embarrassed to admit that he was that 'woman' who'd made the mistakes.

AFTER HE HAD MADE his coffee, he headed to his father's office to read the emails while trying to put the annoyance out of his head. "Hazel, would you like a cup of *kaffe?*"

She smiled and lifted up a cup. "I already got myself one, *denke.*"

He nodded at her annoying efficiency and continued into the office. Once he'd sat down behind his father's desk, he flicked on the computer and waited for it to boot up. It was an old computer and needed upgrading. They'd bought it second hand before they knew how computers worked and how rapidly the technology changed.

When the emails finally loaded, Isaac scrolled through them. Over the weekend, they'd gotten six emails requesting estimates for jobs. It was Isaac's job to get back to them, make appointments, and work out the estimates for the potential customers. They didn't get all the jobs they quoted on, but they got most of them. The small jobs were their bread and butter, but it was with the total kitchen renovations that they brought in the most money per job.

HAZEL KEPT her head down and kept working. She badly needed this job, and she was well aware that all of the Fuller boys were virtually her bosses. If she upset any one of them that could mean her job might be in jeopardy. From how Mr. Fuller had talked about his boys, she had thought they would be younger. Isaac seemed to be in his late twenties and he was still unmarried—she knew that from his clean-shaven face.

From the moment he'd walked in, she knew he was the eldest son, too. He'd held that sense of authority in every mannerism.

She glanced over at Isaac through the glass wall between the offices. He had seemed grumpy and not very friendly, but at least he'd offered her coffee. He couldn't be that bad.

The way his dark hair kicked up and curved over at the middle of his forehead made her smile. It stood up at the front naturally. She knew he, like all the other Amish men, wouldn't have used any products in his hair. Isaac must've been blessed with bouncy hair that naturally grew in a perfect direction. His blue eyes contrasted nicely against his dark skin.

Anyway, she wasn't there to make friends or look at men; she was there to make money for her mother. Mr. Fuller had told her he had seven sons, all of whom worked in his joinery business. From the look and the size of the workshop, she thought the business was doing well. She'd thanked God, and been so grateful to her own bishop for finding Mr. Fuller and this book-keeping job. There had been no jobs whatsoever where she was from, but the Fullers' community was much larger. Her bishop in Allentown had talked to the Fullers' bishop, John Byler, who had kindly offered her a room in their home. The bishop's wife, Ruth, was a tender-hearted lady who'd made her feel at home right away.

After all the devastation she and her mother had been through, Hazel deeply appreciated the kindness both Amish communities had shown her.

It was nearly two hours later when she heard rumbling coming from outside. Then she heard the main door swing open and a group of young men walked in talking loudly and laughing. They all stopped when they saw her.

"Hello, I'm Hazel."

"This is our new bookkeeper *Dat* hired without informing anyone," Isaac said.

She turned around and looked at Isaac, who'd seemingly come out of nowhere. He was clearly still annoyed she was there.

"That's because it's my company and I'm entitled to run it the way I see fit."

Hazel was pleased that Mr. Fuller had come at the same time as the rest of his boys. He'd saved her from an awkward moment. "I'm sorry, Hazel. I had planned to get here before any of them this morning, but I'm not that good at waking early these days. That's why I gave you the key."

Hazel smiled at him and just gave him a little nod, too intimidated by all the boys staring at her.

"Since my boys seem to have lost their tongues, and one of them his manners, I'll introduce them to you. My eldest is Isaac."

"We've already met." Isaac's tone was gruff.

"The next is Levi, and then Joshua, Jacob, Samuel, and Timothy." Mr. Fuller had motioned to each son as he named him. The boys had each smiled and nodded, and some had tipped their hats. "And the youngest is Benjamin."

"Last but not least." Benjamin stepped forward with an outstretched hand.

She giggled at Benjamin. With his good looks and charming manner, he was bound to win many hearts when he grew older. She took Benjamin's hand and shook it and then he stepped back.

"I'm pleased to meet you all. I'll try hard to remember your names."

"Don't worry about theirs,'" Benjamin said as he placed his hand over his heart. "You only need remember mine."

The other brothers chuckled and two of them rolled their eyes.

"Don't take notice of him," one of them said.

"Yeah, most of the time we ignore him," another said.

Their father stepped in between the boys and Hazel, and then he scowled at his sons. "Off to work now."

The boys all walked away except for Isaac. "Can I have a word with you, *Dat?*"

"Right now?"

"Jah."

Hazel noticed Mr. Fuller sigh, and a pained expression appeared on his face as though he didn't want to have this talk with Isaac. "Excuse me, Hazel. I'll be back in one minute."

"Make it a few," Isaac said to Hazel, as he placed a hand on his father's shoulder and moved him away from her. "Let's talk in *your* office, *Dat,* since I no longer appear to have one."

Hazel gulped and looked at father and son walking away. She hadn't known she was sitting in Isaac's place —he'd never said a thing. And, if she was sitting in his office, had she just taken over his job? She placed a hand to her head when she realized what she'd said about their former bookkeeper. Had that been him? If so, that explained why he'd been less than pleased with her being there. She always seemed to say the wrong thing in the wrong time and place. Next time, she'd think before she spoke. Or, maybe better, not say anything.

She went back to her computer screen and focused on the numbers before her. After a couple of minutes, she glanced over at father and son, who seem to be having cross words. Mr. Fuller was still wearing that pained expression and his eyes had glazed over, while Isaac's arms were flailing about in the air. It appeared Isaac was trying his best to explain something to his father, and his father wasn't getting Isaac's point.

She'd been told that Mr. Fuller had a job for her as a bookkeeper. Now she was starting to suspect that he'd created the job especially for her, or more correctly, taken some duties from Isaac and given them to her. Was that it? Had Mr. Fuller been informed of her situation and kind-heartedly created this job?

She didn't mind if Mr. Fuller knew of her situation because that meant either her bishop or Mr. Fuller's bishop had told him. Mr. Fuller would know to keep such things quiet.

CHAPTER 2

*I*saac had closed the door of his father's office before their heated exchange. Now he took a deep breath and waited until his father was seated before he, too, sat down. He tried a calmer approach. "What are you really doing, *Dat?* We agreed we'd keep costs down and that's why I was doing the books. We were keeping expenses down by not employing a bookkeeper." Isaac stared at his father, waiting for him to respond. His father just looked at him blankly. "Aren't you happy with the work I've been doing?"

"I'm more than pleased with your efforts, Isaac, and you should know that."

"*Jah,* I thought I knew that, but then I come here today and find someone sitting in my chair, at my desk, and using my computer. And doing what I understood to be my job. You could, at the very least, have told me, so I wouldn't have gotten a shock when I walked in this morning. When the door was unlocked, my heart about leapt out of my chest. I thought we'd been robbed."

"You're not as easy to talk to since you moved out of home."

"*Dat*, you saw me at the meeting yesterday, and besides that, I only live half a mile away. When did you make the decision to give that girl my job?"

"Here's the thing, Isaac: one day you'll run the business, but right now you don't. This is the business I built from the ground up. It's put food on the table and now it has the capability of providing for all of you boys. *Gott* willing, it will provide for all your brothers' families, and yours, if He keeps blessing us."

This is what his father always did to him. Isaac was already in charge of the day-to-day operations of the business and whenever they were doing well everything was okay, but the minute they had a slight downturn, Isaac knew his father blamed him. The big speech his father was now giving him was designed to pull him back into line and remind him who was boss. He had to respect his father as his elder. Besides, his father was right—it wasn't his business yet.

"I know what you're saying, *Dat*, but the last two years we've grown into the pattern of talking about things before we do anything. And since we've been doing that, things have been going well. You have an idea, or I have an idea, and then we talk about it, we think about it, and then we make a decision. Is there a particular reason why you bypassed discussing something with me this time?"

Mr. Fuller looked over at the young woman and then looked back at Isaac. "She's a bookkeeper and we need one of those. It will free you up to do other things. You're always looking so worried, and even now you've got deep lines in your forehead." Mr. Fuller tapped his own forehead.

"I don't mind the long hours."

"But you're not a trained bookkeeper. We're a growing business, and you can't keep doing all the work you're doing by yourself forever."

"I've read the manual of the software. You just enter the numbers where they tell you to enter them, press a button, and the computer does the rest."

"Hazel can enter the numbers into the software and you can get around to do more quotes and do more quality testing on the boys' work."

"Levi oversees their work."

"You can teach the rest of them what you know. Take one of them to do the quotes with you."

Isaac didn't like that idea. "They'll slow me up."

"Only at first, and then they'll be able to help out. And you don't have to rush through things anymore because Hazel will be entering the numbers."

He glanced over at Hazel. There was a good view of

her through his father's glass-walled office. "Did you tell her this could be a permanent job?"

"What other kind of job is there?"

"What I mean to say is, did you give her a trial period so we can see how she works out?"

His father leaned over, put a hand on his shoulder, and patted him. "Don't worry so much. She'll work out fine. She's done this kind of thing before."

There was nothing else Isaac could say. His father was right. It *was* his business and Isaac knew he couldn't complain, whatever his father did. "Well, where am I going to sit to call back these people?" From his father's desk, he picked up the printouts of the emails that had come in over the weekend. "The only phone was at my desk, and now it's on Hazel's desk."

"You could use that cell phone you use to call back into the office when you're out."

"I don't like using that."

"It's fine. The bishop's given us permission to use it as long as it's for work purposes. Most of our Amish businesses have been given permission to have computers and cells in their offices. We need them to—"

"I know that, *Dat,* but it doesn't get a good signal in this area—that's what I meant. And it's more costly than using the other phone."

"Just pull up a chair to her desk. She won't mind

you being there. It'll only take half an hour to call those people back and make appointments."

Isaac's father was talking to him as though he was strange, but didn't his father realize he'd just given Hazel not only a good chunk of his duties but also his office, desk, chair, computer, and phone? And why would she mind him using the phone for half an hour? His father was talking as though Hazel was more important than he was.

"Fine!" Isaac turned abruptly and walked out of his father's office. His first call would be to the phone company to get another phone line installed. Later he'd think about where to fit another workstation.

It was hard for Isaac, having ninety percent of the responsibility of the business and only ten percent of the say in what happened. Isaac had no idea why his father suddenly thought they required a full-time bookkeeper. He walked into his old office, grabbed a chair from the other side of the room, and pulled it up to his desk. His former desk ... Still she didn't look up. "Excuse me, Hazel."

"Jah?"

"Do you mind if I make some phone calls?"

CHAPTER 3

*H*azel stopped what she was doing and looked across at the man who'd gone from being annoyed by her presence to being borderline hostile. She could sense his rage. "I'm sorry, but have I done something to upset you?"

"I don't have time for a conversation. I've got appointments booked all day and I'll be out on the road soon. I need to make calls now, so I can book more appointments for later in the week."

"Go ahead, don't let me stop you."

He picked up the phone and started making the calls. His demeanor changed as soon as he started talking to the customers. That gave her the impression he was just a typical salesman. As handsome as he was, with a man like that, a woman would never know where she stood.

She jolted herself out of her daydreams about men. With everything that had gone on in her life lately, men should've been the last thing on her mind, but ... there was no harm in looking. The Fuller boys were all handsome, she had to admit that. They were all tall and dark-haired, nice enough looking and solidly built, just the way she liked men to be. Maybe her someday-husband would be like that, and maybe he wouldn't. Looks weren't important to her. All she wanted was someone who would put her needs above his own. In return, she'd do the same. They'd fit together like two pieces of a puzzle. That was her romantic ideal.

She was sure that the man making the phone calls at her desk didn't find her attractive in the least. He was clearly annoyed that she was even there, but the rest of Mr. Fuller's boys had seemed pleased to meet her.

After he'd made his half-dozen calls, he hung up the phone's receiver. "That's all my calls done."

"Oh, are you talking to me?" she asked him.

"*Nee*, I was just saying it out aloud. You can listen if you want."

"*Denke.*" She kept working, determined not to let him bother her. She'd kept things together the last few months, and an angry man was not going to bother her in the least.

"Are you going to answer the phone today?" he asked, peering at her.

"If it rings, I'll answer it." She wondered if that's what he wanted to hear. Mr. Fuller had said nothing about answering the phone. When she considered that she might have sounded rude, she said, "Would you like me to answer the phone?"

"Actually, it might be a good idea. My *vadder* usually answers the phone, but he's not so good with messages. He tends to write things on random slips of paper, and every now and again he loses one with an important phone number."

"I can take messages if that's what you want."

"That would be perfect, *denke*."

Finally, he looked pleased.

"I've looked at your website, so I know the kinds of things you do."

"I'm glad you've looked at the website. There's nothing like being prepared, but I don't want you to answer any questions in case you give the wrong answers. I'm not being rude, it's just that there's a lot to know."

"That's okay, I don't take offense easily. You want me to just take messages, then, and tell them I'll get someone to call them back?"

"That's correct. And I'll be back around lunchtime."

"If someone calls, when will you return their call?"

"If it's important, I've got a cell and you can call me on that. I'll write the number down for you."

"Better than that, I can set the computer up so I can

send you text messages. I can message any of the urgent things to you."

"You can do that?"

"Jah."

"On this?" He reached into a drawer of the desk, pulled the cell phone out, and showed it to her.

"Jah, that's an iPhone. I can set it up from this computer since it's compatible."

"Hmm, I really don't have any idea what you're saying, but if you can text me urgent messages and the numbers of the people I have to call back, I'd appreciate that."

She smiled at him. Maybe they could get along. "Is there anything else you'd like me to do?" As soon as she asked the question, she wished she hadn't. His body immediately stiffened and any trace of a smile was immediately wiped away.

"Nee."

She nodded toward the iPhone. "Can I have that for a moment to set it up?"

"Sure." He handed the phone over. "So, you've always been Amish?"

She giggled. "Always, since I was born. And I guess you have too?"

"Jah. How is it you know so much about phones and computers? Did you learn about them on *rumspringa?"*

"Nee, no *rumspringa* for me. In my last job, we used

computers and cell phones. I worked for a business somewhat similar to this one, only they made Amish furniture. It was a family business, too. My job was to answer phones, update the website, run the blog, and do the bookwork and the payroll."

"I guess *Dat's* given you the payroll too?"

"Not yet, but I can do that if you want me to."

He shook his head as she handed the phone back to him.

"There, it's all set up now," she said.

"That quickly?"

"*Jah*, it only takes a second or two. I just enabled the settings."

"*Denke*, Hazel."

"You're welcome."

He turned and she watched him walk from her small office and out of the building.

Then Mr. Fuller walked out of his office and stood in her doorway. "Don't mind him." He nodded his head in the direction Isaac had gone. "He's a very serious young man. I forgot to tell him you were starting here today. You see, he's not living at home like the other boys, and I thought I had told him."

"He doesn't live at home?"

"He moved out into a *haus* by himself." Mr. Fuller chuckled. "Thought he was too old to live with his parents."

"Oh." Hazel gave a little giggle. "It must have been a shock for him to find me sitting here. I didn't want to get off on the wrong foot with anyone here."

"*Nee*, you won't, don't worry about that. It's my fault. Sometimes I think I've told him things when I haven't." He gave her a smile and walked away, past his office door and out to the back of the workshop.

Around midday, the Fuller boys filed past her office. One of the older ones said, "There's a café down the road and we get lunch from there most days. Would you care to come for a walk with us?"

"*Denke*, but I brought my lunch with me, and also I need to answer the phone."

"Isaac isn't back yet?"

"Not yet."

The young man gave her a smile and joined his brothers. She was sure she'd been speaking to the second oldest one, and she was certain his name was Levi. She hoped, anyway. It was going to take a little time to know all of them.

She wasn't sure where the old Mr. Fuller had gotten to. He was possibly still in the workshop somewhere. Since everyone was taking a break, she figured she'd have her lunch break right there in the office. She leaned down and got her sandwich out of her bag. She'd just taken a big mouthful when Isaac walked back in.

"Have the boys left yet?"

Since her mouth was full, she nodded.

"We have a lunchroom," he said as she swallowed.

"I know, I made myself coffee in there this morning."

"That's right, you did."

"How did things go with the quotes?"

"So far we got the go ahead for one kitchen renovation and one small job."

"Only one job out of the whole six emails?" she asked.

"*Nee.* Out of those six emails, appointments were made for later in the week, and into next week. The *two* jobs I just got were from appointments that had been booked earlier. Anyway, just to get the one kitchen renovation makes it a good day."

She'd annoyed him again. "*Jah*, well, that's good then." She'd opened her big mouth again without thinking. "Would you like me to make you a cup of *kaffe?*"

"Would you?"

"*Jah.* Of course." She stood up and he raised his hand telling her to stop.

"*Nee, denke.* I've already had my limit for the day."

She sat back down. "I thought you meant you'd like a cup."

He shook his head. "I was surprised you would make me one."

"It's not hard." She wasn't sure if he was being deliberately difficult or not.

"I'm fine. *Denke* for the kind offer." He walked away.

CHAPTER 4

*I*saac didn't know what to do with himself. Normally he sat down and made notes on the customer database. *I guess I'll use the old computer in my vadder's office.*

He walked back to Hazel and stuck his head through his former office doorway. "Excuse me, Hazel. Do you know where my *vadder* is?"

"I haven't seen him since just after you left this morning."

Isaac nodded and then walked away. His father would be down back checking on the boys' work. That's where he normally was when he wasn't in his office. He was constantly keeping an eye on everything, making sure they were doing everything correctly and up to his standards.

. . .

At the end of the day, Hazel put the computer into sleep mode and then looked for Mr. Fuller to say goodbye. He had told her that five o'clock was the end of the workday and that's what time she'd arranged for Ruth to collect her. Hazel grabbed her bag from under the desk and headed into Mr. Fuller's office. "Excuse me, Isaac, have you seen your *vadder* anywhere?"

"I think he's gone home."

"Oh. He told me that five o'clock is my finish time. Is it okay for me to go home now?"

"Of course, if that's what he told you."

She didn't want to go through another day of being tense with Isaac. "I hope we'll get along better tomorrow. I know it must've been a shock for you and I'm sorry if I've taken over your office."

"Hazel, it's me who needs to apologize to you. You've done nothing wrong and I've let my irritation with some other things get the better of me. So, I'm sorry."

She smiled and nodded. "Perhaps we should start off with a new day tomorrow?"

"Very good." He gave her a little nod and then looked back at the computer.

"Goodbye."

"Goodbye, Hazel."

She was pleased she'd had that talk with him. It made her feel better. They were probably never going to get along very well together, but as long as they could be civil to each other that was fine.

When Hazel walked outside, she saw Ruth's buggy and hurried to it. She climbed onto the seat next to Ruth.

"*Denke*, Ruth. It's very nice of you to do this for me."

"It's no bother. As I said, I'm always out and about doing one thing or another for John. If ever I can't collect you, I'll have John or one of the boys fetch you."

Bishop John and his wife Ruth had a large family, but their children had grown up and left home. Hazel had met one of the older sons the previous night; he'd helped her bring her bags into the house.

"How was your first day?"

"I think it went really well. Mr. Fuller seemed pleased with me."

"That's good. I hope it all works out well for you."

"It's looking like it so far."

Ruth gave her a sidelong glance. "The Fuller boys didn't give you any trouble, did they?"

Hazel giggled. "They were all very friendly. Just like their *vadder*." She wasn't about to mention the friction with Isaac, and especially not to the bishop's wife.

Dinner that night at Bishop John's house was interrupted by two different sets of visitors. Ruth told her that it was always like that. People were constantly dropping by unexpectedly. Hazel kept herself busy by helping Ruth wherever she could, and after the visitors left, Hazel went to bed exhausted. She wasn't just physically tired, she was also mentally tired. She'd been tense and on edge all day, hoping she would get along with everyone at work.

When Hazel finally put her head on the soft pillow, she thanked God for the opportunity that had been given to her. Like she did every night, she also prayed for her mother to recover. It would take a while before she could pray for her father after what he'd done. She knew the scriptures said to pray for people who had wronged you, but she still couldn't do it. He'd never been a real father to her or a decent husband to her mother. He hadn't cared about either of them.

Now, after he'd left them again, and this time for an *Englisch* woman, the shock of it was too much for her mother and *Mamm* had ended up having a breakdown. Now her mother was in a treatment facility. If it weren't for Aunt Bee, her mother's sister, organizing everything, Hazel wouldn't have gotten the job and a place to live, and her mother wouldn't be getting the help she needed. Beatrice, always known as Bee with no A, was helping with the medical bills too, but there was only so far that their money could stretch.

It'd been another stressful day working in the family business. With all of the responsibility, the limited decision-making, and someone always looking over his shoulder, Isaac felt under constant pressure.

Monday and Thursday nights were his times with Mary Lou, his girlfriend. Mary Lou had insisted on seeing him two nights a week as well as during the weekends. To save time on those nights, he collected her from the bakery where she worked part time. Their routine was simply that they'd have dinner together somewhere in town, and then he'd take her home.

It was just after five thirty when he arrived to collect her. She was sitting on the seat at the bus stop across the road from the bakery. He stopped the buggy just after the bus stop. It was always a pleasure to see Mary Lou's bright smiling face. She was a small girl with dark hair and blue eyes, coloring that was very similar to his own.

They'd been together for two years. The first year was enjoyable, but for the last year Mary Lou had talked constantly of marriage. Isaac couldn't blame her, not really. It was only a normal thing for a woman to want to be married after she became a certain age, but since he'd moved into the house by himself, he found he delighted in his own company. Coming from a rowdy houseful of boys, the silence was something he now craved. He wasn't ready to give that up, not for Mary Lou, not for anybody.

Mary Lou jumped into the front seat. "Did you see

her?" Her blue eyes sparkled and her cheeks were flushed rosy pink.

"See who?" Hearing a bus coming, he moved his horse forward, so it would be well out of the way.

"The girl who's living at the bishop's *haus*. I heard she's working for you."

"Hazel?"

"*Jah*. Hazel Bauer, they said her name was. So, it's true?"

"I wasn't aware she was living at the bishop's *haus*. If I'd been told that, I'd forgotten it. Maybe I did know."

She gave him a playful shove. "You're so forgetful, Isaac."

"She's actually living there permanently, then, or is she just staying there until she finds another place?"

"I don't know. I thought you'd know. Penny came into the bakery today and she was at the bishop's *haus* last night and Hazel was there. No one seems to know anything about her and Penny said that Ruth was funny about answering questions about her. It seems she's a real mystery."

He didn't like the way Mary Lou had to know everything about everybody. But he knew that's what some women were like. *Nobody's perfect,* he told himself. He had to admit he was curious, too.

"Is she pretty?"

He glanced over at Mary Lou. If he told her Hazel was pretty, she could get jealous. On the other hand, if he told her that she wasn't pretty, that would be a lie. "Some men might find her pretty." He kept his eyes on the road ahead, feeling pleased with himself for his clever answer and not giving anything away.

"What would you say? What's your opinion of her?"

"I would say that there's only one woman I look at in that way, and that's you."

She put her hand up to her mouth and giggled. "What's she doing at your work? What kind of work is she doing?"

"Bookwork and accounting-type duties. She's taken over those tasks from me. She'll end up doing invoices, payroll, and that kind of thing. It's about time we had someone do that so I can get on with other things."

She pouted. "Why didn't you tell me someone was starting at the workshop?"

"Because I didn't know myself until this morning. My *vadder* forgot to tell me. I walked in and was shocked to see her this morning."

She slowly nodded, as though she accepted his answer, albeit reluctantly. "Where are we going tonight?"

"The same place. Is that alright?"

Mary Lou was quiet for a while before she said, "That's okay."

"Would you rather go someplace else?" They had gotten into the habit of going to Downtown Diner. Because Mary Lou had insisted on going out two nights a week, if they went to a nice restaurant it would end up being far too expensive. The diner had good food and was reasonably priced.

"I was just hoping tonight might be a special night, that's all."

He knew that Mary Lou was hoping that he would ask her to marry him. It was a roundabout hint—a little nudge.

"Isn't every night we're together special?" he asked.

"Jah, it is. It just makes me feel funny that you've got someone working for you that I've never met."

"That's easily solved. Come in tomorrow and meet her. You'll like her, she's very friendly."

She twisted her body toward him. "Friendly ... She's not too friendly with you, is she?"

He chuckled. "*Nee*, just normal friendly."

"Is that supposed to make me feel better?"

He breathed out heavily. "Mary Lou, you're sounding like you're a little jealous."

"I'm not. I'm just worried, that's all."

"You're worried about Hazel?"

After a moment of silence, she said, *"Nee*, it's not just her."

"Well, what is it, or who is it?" As soon as he asked the question, he wished he hadn't. He could sense what was coming.

"We hold the record for the longest engaged couple in the community. I feel like we're becoming a joke."

"A joke? To whom?"

She shook her head. "Forget it."

"Nee, you said it, so it must be bothering you."

"It is. I mean, it's sort of a joke that we haven't gotten married. People are sniggering about us. The couple who are together but never marry, that kind of thing."

"I don't think anyone's saying that."

"Well, it's true."

"Just give me some more time, that's all I need."

"Time to do what? Is it that you're not sure about me? Do you think someone else might come along who suits you better?"

"Nee, none of those things."

"How long are you going to have me wait?"

"Not long. Only a few more months."

She groaned. "It's always just a few more months."

"Nee, it's not. I don't believe I've ever said that."

"You did." She crossed her arms over her chest. "Three years ago, you said it would just be another three months."

"I'm sorry." Then he said, "We've only been together for two years."

"Is that all you can say?"

"Look, I've had a hard day. Can we talk about this another time?"

"Nee, I think we should talk about it now. Two years will turn into three, and then—"

"Okay, give me four more weeks and then we'll talk about things further."

"What exactly will we talk about?"

He groaned inwardly. Getting married was the eventual outcome. "A wedding." He couldn't blame her for wanting to get married. They'd been happy enough together, so he knew their marriage would be a happy one.

"Our wedding? We'll talk about our wedding?"

He nodded. "Just give me a few more weeks to get used to the idea."

"I don't want to force you into it. If you don't want to marry me, just let me know."

"I do want to."

"Are you sure?" she asked.

"*Jah.*"

"*Gut.* Four weeks, you said?"

He glanced over at her. "Well, *jah,* and that's what you just said."

"*Jah,* four weeks." She flashed him a smile. "I'll give you four weeks."

"Now let's talk about something else and enjoy our time together."

Mary Lou nodded. "Okay."

He was a little annoyed that she'd forced him into a corner, but tried his best to hide it. He knew Mary Lou would make a good wife. It was the timing that was all wrong. How would he handle having a wife, and soon children, along with all the pressure of the family business? The only thing that kept him calm after the daily struggles with his father was going home to a peaceful house with nothing but the floorboards to squeak under his feet, the rustle of the leaves in the trees as they swayed in the night's breeze, and the song of the birds in the morning.

He'd never considered being a bachelor forever until he'd moved out of his family home. If he never married, he now knew, that would be okay. He could cook well enough to make the basic meals for himself and that's all he needed. He knew *Gott* had planned out his life already and He'd designed man and woman to be together. Marrying Mary Lou might be the best thing for him.

Over a steak sandwich dinner that night, Hazel's name came up again.

"What if there's some scandal she's trying to run away from?"

"Are we talking about Hazel again?"

"Jah. See what you can find out and let me know."

Isaac drew back. "I hope you're joking. I'll do no such thing."

"Don't you want to know what kind of person you have working for you? She's the only person who's ever worked there that isn't a family member, isn't that so?"

"That's right."

"And what do you know about her, again?"

He looked at the area of his sandwich where he planned to take his next bite. "Very little."

"Doesn't that worry you?"

"I trust my *vadder's* judgment."

"It doesn't matter. I guess I'll see her at the next meeting and then I can get to know her."

"Like I said, why don't you stop by tomorrow and introduce yourself? If she's just moved here she could do with some friends, I'm guessing."

Mary Lou's face lit up. "You really wouldn't mind if I stopped by and said hello to the new girl?"

"*Nee,* I don't mind at all. I think she's your age, or thereabouts."

"I can't wait to meet her and find out exactly what's going on with her and why she's moved here."

"I can't figure out why you're so interested."

"Only because no one knows about her, that's the only reason. She's a mystery. She works for you and you don't even know anything about her."

"That's because my *vadder* employed her. If I had employed her, I would've found out everything about her."

"There's your answer, then."

He was just about to take another bite of his sandwich, but he stopped. "Answer to what?"

"Your *vadder* must know about her. Otherwise, why would he have given her the job?"

"I guess you're right." Just so she wouldn't keep

asking him, he said, "He certainly didn't tell me anything about her." He took another bite of his sandwich. The diner made the best steak sandwiches. The meat was tender, the bread thick and fresh, and there was just the right amount of sauce.

As they were driving back to Mary Lou's house in the buggy, his mind traveled back to one of his father's suggestions of earlier that day. Perhaps he wouldn't be so stressed if he shared his duties with one of his brothers. He could take Levi with him for a couple of weeks when he was quoting for jobs and pitching for new business. It made sense that someone beside himself and his father could perform that function. If not Levi, one of his other brothers would be suited for that job. And when Benjamin got a little older, he was going to make a great salesman.

"We're here already," Mary Lou said as he stopped the buggy outside her house.

"Here we are, on another Monday night."

"In four weeks' time, maybe things will be different." She fluttered her lashes at him.

He laughed. *"Gut nacht,* Mary Lou."

"Denke for a lovely dinner." She took him by surprise when she quickly leaned over and gave him a kiss on the cheek. Then she jumped down from the buggy and hurried through the darkness toward her house.

"*Gut nacht,*" he said, quietly answering himself even though no one could hear him.

He turned his buggy around and headed back down her driveway. Mary Lou was a good choice for a wife, he reminded himself. They never had disagreements, and now that he'd made a timeline for asking her to marry him, he had to get things at work in order. His father had been right; having someone there like Hazel would be a good thing for the business.

CHAPTER 5

The next morning, Hazel was engrossed in trying to correct errors when Isaac walked in and stood in front of her desk.

"Hello, Hazel."

He was so handsome and tall. "Good morning, Isaac."

"I hope you don't mind, but I suggested to my girlfriend that she come in and introduce herself to you sometime today."

For some reason, she was a little surprised that he had a girlfriend. Even though he was handsome, he was so rigid and awkward and he barely smiled. "That was very thoughtful, *denke*. I don't really know anybody in the community yet, apart from your family and Ruth and the bishop, and one of their sons." She wasn't sure how long she would be staying in the community and wasn't too keen on getting to know people very well, but his offer was a kind one.

"I suggested she come about lunchtime."

"Well, I'll be here."

"Very good." He walked away from her, leaving her to work through the errors he'd previously made in the accounting system.

She noticed he headed to the lunchroom and then came back out with a mug of coffee. After that, he sat in his father's office, next to hers. They were separated by a large glass wall. People from either office had a good view of who was coming in the doorway, but only after they'd taken a few steps inside.

The way the offices were arranged wasn't convenient for customers or for whomever was supposed to greet the customers, but Mr. Fuller had informed her that customers rarely came to the workshop. In fact, they were encouraged not to. Isaac carried a full range of samples with him, eliminating the need for foot traffic within the factory.

She wondered what his girlfriend was like and how long they'd been together. He certainly looked old enough to be married by now, and have a few young children.

An hour later, Isaac's brothers came into the office, and one by one they greeted her. Benjamin was last and handed her a single flower.

"*Denke,* Benjamin. That was thoughtful. It's so lovely." She heard sniggers from some of his brothers.

Benjamin ignored them. "Would you like me to put it in water for you?"

"*Jah, denke,* and then you can place it right here on my desk."

One of the brothers chimed in, "You can think of Benjamin every time you look at it."

She giggled as Benjamin gave him a shove. The boys quickly dispersed toward the workshop when their father came in behind them.

At the same time, Isaac walked out of his father's office. "What's going on?" he asked.

"The boys are just having a bit of fun, that's all," Joshua, the third eldest, said over his shoulder as he walked away.

"The workplace is no place for fun." Mr. Fuller put his hands on his hips and his lips downturned into a frown. "Get to work, the lot of you."

By this time, Benjamin was hurrying back to her with the flower in a glass of water.

"What's this?" Isaac asked, staring at the flower.

"It's an unusual and beautiful flower that I saw in *Mamm's* garden. I thought it belonged with Hazel."

Isaac shook his head. "Well, give it to her and then get to work."

Hazel had no choice but to watch the scene unfold.

She saw Mr. Fuller doing his best to hide an amused smirk as his youngest son placed the flower on her desk. *"Denke,* Benjamin. That will surely brighten my day."

Benjamin flashed her a big smile and then walked past Mr. Fuller who was still in the doorway of her office along with Isaac.

"How is everything going?" Mr. Fuller asked her.

"Really well."

"That's good. If there's anything you need, just let me know."

"Denke."

"If ever Ruth can't fetch you from work or bring you here, just let me know and I'll have one of the boys give you a ride."

She nodded. "That's very kind of you, Mr. Fuller. *Denke.* I'll remember that."

Mr. Fuller and Isaac left her alone.

THE MORNING FOLLOWED the same pattern as the one before. After making his phone calls at her desk, Isaac left the office. At midday, after the boys walked out to get their lunch, Hazel pulled out her sandwich, unwrapped it, and took a quick bite. She'd barely swallowed her mouthful when a young Amish woman walked up to her office. Hazel smiled at her and placed her sandwich down on the wrapper.

The young woman looked at her, smiled too, and then walked forward. "Hello, you must be Hazel."

Hazel stood up and offered her hand. *"Jah,* and you're Isaac's girlfriend?"

"I am."

"He mentioned you were going to stop by." Hazel figured that his girlfriend matched him perfectly. He was a good-looking man, and Mary Lou was fair skinned, dark-haired, blue-eyed, and very pretty.

"Do you mind if I sit?" Mary Lou asked.

"Please do."

She sat in the same chair that Isaac had used earlier that morning and pulled it closer to the desk. "What brings you to our community, Hazel?"

"This job, for one thing." Hazel didn't want the conversation to be all about herself. "And do you work?"

"I only have a part-time job at a bakery. I mostly help my *mudder* at home. I've got many younger sisters and brothers." She gave a little giggle. "We're quite busy."

"I guess you would be. I'm the only one in the family—only child."

Mary Lou raised her eyebrows. "That is highly unusual. I barely know any Amish family who has just one child."

Hazel nodded. "I know, but that's just how it is." Out of the corner of her eye, she could see her sandwich. She was very hungry, but she couldn't eat in front of Mary Lou because that would be rude. Neither did she have an extra sandwich to be able to offer her one. "Can I make you a cup of coffee or something?"

"That would be nice. I'll come with you. I've been here several times and I know where the lunchroom is."

Soon they were sitting in the lunchroom, waiting for the teakettle to boil.

Mary Lou looked around. "It's very quiet in here. Where is everybody?"

"I'm not sure where Mr. Fuller is. He's got to be around here somewhere, and the boys have gone up the road for lunch."

"What about Isaac?"

"I don't think he's come back yet from his morning appointments." Hazel stood and pulled two cups out of the cupboard.

"I suppose you're wondering why Isaac and I aren't married. He's literally devoted to me, you see."

Hazel turned around to stare at Mary Lou. "I generally don't worry too much about what's going on in the lives of others. I stay out of other people's business."

Mary Lou giggled. "I know, but you're a woman and I thought you'd have to wonder."

She shook her head. "I barely know the Fuller family at all."

"It's a secret, that's all."

"You're in a secret relationship with Isaac?" She knew that wasn't true because he had openly called Mary Lou his girlfriend.

Mary Lou giggled again but this time a little more high-pitched. "I don't mean *that*. It's a secret that we're getting married, and we haven't told anybody yet."

"Ah, well that is good news. The best kind of news."

"Denke. It's so hard to have the news and not be able to tell anybody."

"You just told me."

"I've only told you because you don't know anybody here yet. So, I was just giving you a broad overview of how things work."

Now it was clear why Mary Lou was there. She was warning her off her boyfriend. Hazel was disappointed; she could've used a real friend at a time like this. She'd grown up without friends because of her father's behavior. No one in the community wanted their daughters to associate with her or her family. "I can assure you that while I'm here I'm just concentrating on my job."

"And that's just as it should be. If you came to the community looking for a husband, Isaac has many brothers. You look like you're around twenty?"

"I'm twenty-six."

Mary Lou opened her eyes wide. Everyone thought Hazel was younger than she was.

"The closest to you in age would be Levi. He would

be a wonderful choice for you. Oh, but he already has a girlfriend and she's my good friend, Lucy. I'm sure they'll get married."

"*Denke*, but I'm not looking for a husband. I've got too many other things going on in my life at the moment."

Mary Lou leaned forward. "Such as?" Then Mary Lou giggled. "Forgive me. We hardly know one another. I came here to invite you to the quilting bee tomorrow. Us ladies have such fun and then we eat baked goods afterward."

"*Denke*, that's very kind, but I've got work."

"Oh, silly me. That's right. You wouldn't be able to come, would you?"

"*Nee.*" The kettle boiled and Hazel made coffee for herself and Mary Lou, and then she sat down opposite Mary Lou at the small wooden table.

"I have a job too, like I said, but I don't work there every day. I work in a bakery, but we have a few tables and we serve coffee, so I suppose it's more of a café."

"I'm glad you stopped by because I won't feel so nervous now when I go to the meetings. At least I'll know someone."

"But you're staying with the bishop, aren't you?"

"I am. And since they have so many visitors, I'm meeting a few people at their *haus*, but it's nice to meet someone about my own age."

"I'm glad. That's what I said to Isaac. I said, the poor

girl probably knows no one, so I must stop by and say hello."

"It's very kind of you to think about me." She took a sip of her coffee, not knowing whether the woman in front of her was a friend or a foe.

"So, what do you think of Isaac?"

It was a surprising question, and there was no correct way to answer that. She didn't want Mary Lou to think she was interested in Isaac and yet she couldn't say anything rude to offend her. She tried to be as tactful as she could. "He's very dedicated to his job."

"I know that, but did he mention me?"

"*Jah*, he did this morning when he said you were coming in to see me."

"What did you think when you first saw him?"

Hazel laughed. "Well that's a funny story. He didn't know I was starting work yesterday, his *vadder* forgot to tell him, and naturally he was surprised to see me when he came in."

"*Jah*, but what did you think of him? Do you think he's handsome?"

"All the Fuller boys are handsome." She could see that her saying that disturbed Mary Lou. Hazel further explained, "When I first met him, I thought he was stiff and unapproachable, but then I found I was wrong because he's polite and friendly. Anyway, I can tell he's devoted to you."

"Do you think so?"

Hazel nodded. *"Jah.* His face lit up just when he was talking about you."

"Oh, I didn't know."

She didn't seem confident in their relationship and Hazel wondered why. "When did you say you were getting married?"

"You must never mention that. That information is not out yet."

"I know. I remember you said that, and I would never mention it. I'm just asking *you* and no one can hear us."

"In about four weeks we'll tell everybody."

"That will be exciting."

"You don't have a boyfriend where you come from?"

"There's been a lot going on in my life lately and a boyfriend wouldn't fit in with … No, I haven't."

"Why? What happened?"

She shook her head. "I can't really say because it's not really about me."

Mary Lou leaned forward. "You have a secret?"

Hazel shook her head. *"Nee,* it's nothing like that."

Now frown lines marred Mary Lou's forehead. "Well, why can't you tell me?"

"I'd rather keep quiet about things."

"Does Isaac know your secret?"

Now Mary Lou was focused on her having a secret; this wasn't good. She'd talked herself into a corner and she had no idea how to get out of it. She placed her coffee down on the table and wrapped her hands around the mug. "It's truly nothing."

"If it's nothing, tell me what it is."

"Ah, Mary Lou. It's nice to see you."

Both girls turned to see Mr. Fuller standing in the doorway of the lunchroom.

"Hello, Mr. Fuller. I just stopped by to meet Hazel."

"Very good."

"Would you like me to make you a cup of *kaffe* or anything, Mr. Fuller?" Hazel asked.

"That would be nice *denke*, Hazel. I'll be in my office until Isaac comes back and kicks me out." A small smile twitched at his lips, and then he walked away.

Hazel stood to make his coffee.

"That's right, you're in Isaac's office. How will he get his work done?"

"I didn't know I was in his office until later yesterday. Isaac has been using his *vadder's* computer and using the phone on my desk to make his calls. He's organizing another phone line."

"You're sharing the office with him?"

"Not really. Well, maybe, sort of, for half an hour a day until the new phone line is installed."

"I do hope we can be friends, Hazel."

"*Jah*, I'd like that.

"You don't work Saturdays, do you?"

"*Nee*, I don't. I only work Monday through Friday."

"Perhaps we could do something together this Saturday?"

"I would like that, but unfortunately, I have to do something this Saturday."

"Maybe the Saturday after?"

"Jah, maybe."

"We'll arrange something. What kind of things do you like to do?"

She poured Mr. Fuller's coffee while she thought about it. There wasn't really anything she liked to do. Hazel didn't really have any hobbies. She did like to take long walks, but that seemed a silly thing to say to Mary Lou, and it wasn't really considered a hobby by most people. "I don't know, just the usual things. If you'll excuse me a moment, I'll just take this coffee to Mr. Fuller."

When she got to Mr. Fuller's office, he was reading something and she placed the mug on his desk.

"Denke, Hazel."

"You're welcome." She hurried back to Mary Lou. When she got back to the lunchroom, Mary Lou's mug was in the sink, empty, and Mary Lou was standing by the sink.

"I must go. It was very nice to meet you, Hazel, and let's do something together soon."

"I'd like that."

"Perhaps I should arrange something with my friends?"

Hazel nodded. "That sounds like fun. I'd like that."

"We can all go out to dinner one night."

"Okay."

"Leave it up to me, and I'll arrange it." Without saying goodbye, Mary Lou turned and walked out.

Hazel was glad that at least Mary Lou had left with a smile, and that she had managed to convince Mary Lou that she wasn't after her boyfriend. Hazel guessed many girls were attracted to Isaac, which had probably given Mary Lou cause for concern in the past.

CHAPTER 6

Isaac was just about to enter the factory when Mary Lou stepped outside.

"Ah, this is a surprise," he said.

She looked up and smiled. "Hello. I've just paid a visit to Hazel."

"*Gut*. She should get to know some people around here apart from my brothers. Benjamin has taken a particular interest and I don't want Hazel to be scared away." He laughed.

"She's not the kind of girl I imagined you might have working here."

"Why not?"

"She doesn't seem to be a very loyal employee."

Her words struck him as odd. He saw nothing wrong with Hazel. What had she done? "Why do you say that?"

"Because of what she said about you."

"Me?"

Mary Lou nodded. "Stiff and unapproachable, that's what she said you were."

"Really?" Isaac wasn't happy that the new employee was talking about him like that. "I thought she would've had more respect for me than that."

"Don't be too annoyed. It was just girls' talk. I asked her if she thought you were handsome and she said what she said." Mary Lou giggled again, but Isaac didn't see the funny side of anything.

"I don't know why you girls have to talk about people like that. Did you have to say anything about me at all?"

"She said it, not me. And I can tell you right now that she's hiding something. She's got a secret and she's as good as said it to me. She's only here because of some secret. Probably a dark family secret because she said the secret wasn't hers."

"What do you think it is?"

"She wouldn't tell me. It has to do with the reason she's here, though."

"And it annoyed you because you didn't find out what it is?"

"Nee, because it's a secret. Your *vadder* would know. Why don't you just ask him what she's doing here?"

"If she's got a secret, it's not of my concern. I told you that last night. It's only my concern if it affects her ability to work. She's only been here a day and she's done a great job so far."

"You can't tell if she's a good worker after only just one and a half days."

"I think I can. She's a quick learner, a hard worker, and efficient. She's taken a lot of my duties from me and there's a lot of pressure off my shoulders. My *vadder* did the right thing in employing a bookkeeper."

"I could've learned to do the bookkeeping. I still can. I've always been good with numbers. It won't take me long to learn and that will keep all the jobs within the family. Then you wouldn't have to employ a stranger. She can go back where she came from and take her secret with her."

Isaac frowned at Mary Lou. It wasn't a kind thing to say, not at all, and he'd always seen her as kind-hearted. "She's not a stranger now."

She playfully dug Isaac in the ribs. "You know what I mean."

He stepped away. *"Denke* for stopping by and saying hello to her. I'm sure that has made her feel more at ease. I'll see you on Thursday night."

"Okay. Bye." Mary Lou walked away without waiting for him to say goodbye.

He watched her leave and figured he'd offended her in some way. He didn't like to be poked in the ribs. He never liked it when she shoved and poked him. It was annoying. Putting Mary Lou out of his mind, he walked into the workshop.

LATER THAT NIGHT, Isaac had just finished dinner and the whole time his mind had been on his relationship with Mary Lou. He'd made himself a simple meal of chops and vegetables. The vegetables were always the same: peas, carrots, and mashed potatoes.

Just because they got along fine, there was no compelling reason to get married. He wasn't in love with Mary Lou, but then again, what was love? Many said love grew after marriage and it didn't matter who you married, but since he was happy being on his own, he realized that he was rethinking the whole marriage idea.

When Isaac was just finishing washing up the dishes, he heard the rumblings of a buggy. He guessed it was one of his brothers come to get away from the noisy household. Then, through the kitchen window, he saw his mother get out of the buggy. She rarely went out on her own at night. In fact, she never did.

He ran out to meet her. "*Mamm*, is something wrong?"

She laughed. "Well, there *is* something wrong if a *mudder* can't talk to her own son—her firstborn."

"You've just come to visit me? You had me worried.

In all the time I've lived here, you've never visited me at night."

"I had a visit from Mary Lou today."

He put his arm around his mother's shoulders. "Let's get you inside out of the cold."

When they were sitting in the living room by the crackling warmth of the fire, his mother said, "I never asked this before, but I have wondered. Why is it that you haven't married Mary Lou yet? She's a lovely girl and you get along with her so well."

Mary Lou had obviously thought that by getting his mother onside, the path to their marriage would be speeded up. That annoyed him, since he had said he needed a few weeks and she'd agreed with that. "I intend to marry her one day, but right now, I'm enjoying living by myself and that's what I'm doing. I'm not going with the crowd and marrying by the time I'm twenty-two in some kind of a fearsome panic."

"We all know you're not going to marry at twenty-two because you're way past that age now. I think you're being harsh."

"Why is that harsh?"

"Not only that, it doesn't make sense."

"It makes perfect sense to me," he said. Now he was annoyed with Mary Lou for worrying his mother and causing her to make the trip to see him at night.

"Mary Lou might not wait forever."

He sighed. "If she loves me, she'll wait. If a woman loves a man, they'll both wait until the time is right."

"People in love don't want to wait. That's what concerns me and I wouldn't mind saying I think it's concerning a certain young lady."

He raised his eyebrows. "Did Mary Lou put you up to this? Is that why you're here?"

"*Ach nee,* she never said anything. She stops by every week and we have a nice little chat."

He grumbled, "About me, I suppose?"

"About you, and about other things. Not just about you."

He wasn't totally convinced about that. "Would you like a hot tea, *Mamm?*"

"*Jah,* I would like some tea." She followed him into the kitchen.

"*Mamm,* I'm not being rude, and I'm pleased that you came to visit me, but is there anything in particular that you have come to say? Or are you and Mary Lou just trying to speed up the process of me getting married? I can tell you this, I'm not a person who folds under pressure; if anything it will push the marriage back further."

She sat down at the small wooden kitchen table. "I'm concerned, that's all. And I haven't said anything up till now, but I think the time has come. And then I got to thinking, maybe Mary Lou isn't the right one for you and that's why—"

He interrupted, "Normally, you might be right. What you said probably makes sense, but you're wrong. I suppose you've heard about the new girl at work?"

"I have heard a little, and I know that her name is Hazel Bauer."

"*Jah*, so … are you thinking she would suit me better? Is that why you're here?"

Her eyebrows rose. "I met her at the bishop's *haus* with your *vadder*. I was there when she was offered the job. She's lovely, but I never once thought that she'd suit you. Now, I think it odd that you'd even be considering the new girl as your *fraa* when you have a lovely girlfriend already."

He shook his head and smiled. "Wait a moment. The thought about marrying the new girl never entered my head. I thought that maybe *you* thought that."

"I never thought that. Although I think it a little strange that you'd think that I thought it."

He sat down with her while waiting for the water to boil. He noticed she was trying not to laugh. "Oh no, *Mamm*. Don't you start."

She laughed, and when she stopped, she said, "I don't know why I'm laughing."

"Me either, but over the years I've noticed you always laugh before you get very serious. I'm feeling a stern lecture coming on."

"I don't know about a lecture, but I do want to talk with you about something."

"I knew it."

"It's not a lecture." His mother tugged at the strings of her prayer *kapp*.

"Go on, what is it?"

"I never interfere in your life. Not since you've grown up. But now I'm thinking I should've, and now I'm going to speak my mind about something."

"What have I done?" He wondered if he'd stepped across the line and spoken to his father rudely about him employing Hazel, or was it regarding Mary Lou and her visit to his mother? Mary Lou's visit to her had to have been directly after Mary Lou had spoken to Hazel.

"It's unfair. She's been waiting so long, and it's just unfair. What if you keep her waiting longer and then you change your mind? She'll be much older and all the potential suitors will be married and she'll have no one."

"I will marry Mary Lou, I'm just not ready yet. If you must know, we talked about this just recently, Mary Lou and me. She's fine with things. I explained everything to her. That's why I wondered why she had the need to say anything to you after we'd just talked about things."

"*Nee,* she hasn't."

"Really?"

His mother nodded.

"Why do you have this on your mind so much today?" he asked.

"It's not just today, it's been on my mind for some time. I haven't said anything up until now, but how much longer are you going to make that poor girl wait? What if all your brothers follow your example and don't marry until they're nearly thirty?"

"They won't. My brothers and I are nothing alike. Well, most of them are nothing like me. I'm a grown man, *Mamm,* so I'm quite surprised you're saying these things to me."

"You might be a grown man, but I'm always going to be your *mudder* and now I'm telling you what I think you should do. I've held my tongue long enough."

The kettle boiled and he filled a teapot, let it steep, and poured himself and his mother each a cup of tea. Once he'd done that, he sat down with her. He watched his mother take a sip of tea and waited to find out what else was on her mind. "Is that all you've come to say to me?"

"That's all."

"Okay, good." He sipped his tea. "I was shocked *Dat* had employed someone without discussing it with me, but I think it's a really good thing. She's working out really well."

"That's good, I'm glad. She seems a nice girl."

"You said you were there when she was offered the job?"

"Jah, and that was at the bishop's *haus* when your *vadder* told the bishop he had a job which would suit her."

"Ach gut." His mumbles were full of sarcasm. "No one ever tells me anything anymore, it seems. How did it all come about?"

"We were visiting Bishop John and Ruth on Sunday afternoon and then they had Hazel staying there with them. She'd just moved in that day. They've got so many rooms now, and I think Ruth gets lonely. She hasn't ever said anything, but that's what I think. You see, John had told Hazel that he'd find her a job because she couldn't find one where she'd come from. There were no jobs."

"Ah, so she didn't move here specifically for the job with us?"

"Nee. And I can't say more than that." She drew her lips tightly together.

"So, there's more to tell?"

"I can't say anything."

He pushed the teacup and saucer away from himself. This is what women always did. His mother wanted to tell him what else she knew about Hazel, but knew she shouldn't. By dropping little hints, she wanted him to keep asking more and begging her to tell him. He resisted asking anything further even though he wanted to learn more. Mary Lou insisting Hazel had a secret had intrigued him.

"Did Mary Lou put you up to this?"

"*Nee*, it was my idea to talk with you."

"*Gut*. Otherwise I'd feel ganged up on."

His mother giggled. "That would be terrible. A big strong man being ganged up on by two small women."

"Small in stature, and that's all," he said. "Large in producing fear in men."

She smiled at him and then looked around his kitchen. "You've done a good job of living by yourself. This looks like a proper kitchen."

He chuckled. "It is a proper kitchen, and I have proper knives and forks, plates and cups, and even food."

"You've done well without a woman to look after you."

"*Denke,* I think."

"I should get back to your *vadder*. I've got the younger boys washing up and cleaning the kitchen."

"Really?"

"*Jah,* it won't hurt them."

"I know that, but you never made me do it."

"You were always out helping your *vadder*. '*Dat's* little helper' is what we used to call you."

"Yeah, I remember."

"Ahh, it would've been nice to have a *dochder* or two, maybe three. For some reason, *Gott* kept giving me boys. When you got older, I made myself happy with the thought of you marrying and then I'd have a *dochder*-in-law, but I'm still waiting."

"If you've given up on me and Mary Lou, there's always Levi and Lucy."

"We'll see what happens there. I'm not convinced about that pairing."

Isaac didn't ask why she felt that way, preferring not to know. With private and personal knowledge came the burden of being careful not to repeat it.

"Where would you live if Mary Lou and you got married?"

"Right here. There's nothing wrong with this place."

"I know, it's lovely."

Isaac knew his mother was dropping subtle hints, trying to move him forward with his plans. "Don't worry, *Mamm,* you'll be the first to know when I ask Mary Lou to marry me."

"Denke. That's just the way it should be."

"You have my word."

"Well, I've said what I've come to say, and now all there is left for me to do is go home and make your *vadder* a cup of hot tea before bedtime." She pushed herself to her feet and he stood as well.

"I'll walk you out. You really shouldn't have come out on your own like this."

"Why? Do you think I'm too old?"

"Nee, not at all. You're capable of doing all kinds of things."

She chuckled as she walked through the front doorway with him following. When they got to the buggy, he leaned down and gave his mother a kiss on the cheek before she got into the buggy. It often amazed him how, at five feet and two inches, she could have such tall sons. Even his father was only five feet eight and yet he and all of his brothers were over six feet tall.

"Gut nacht."

"Gut nacht, Mamm."

He watched the buggy disappear into the dark night, then slowly walked back into his house.

CHAPTER 7

That night in bed, Isaac asked himself about the real reason he'd delayed taking his relationship with Mary Lou further. He wondered if it was anything deep in the recesses of his mind that was causing him to resist marriage. The only thing he could think of besides liking his own company was that girl he'd met when he was a young teen. He couldn't share that with his mother because she would say it wasn't a real thing to think genuine love could be so whimsical, but that girl had made the biggest impact on him when it came to love.

It was many years ago while his family was on vacation that he and his brothers had played with the local Amish children. He'd become intrigued with a girl called Livy, and they'd gravitated toward one another as though there was a magnetic attraction. They had left the group and walked alone in the woods. The other children were close, he remembered, because they could hear their laughter nearby. In his eyes, the green-eyed beauty was perfect. In his childish naivety, he'd talked to her about marriage, and she'd agreed to marry him when they both grew up. After their walk they re-joined the others. And after that day, he never saw her again.

Now that he was older, he knew that he'd never find that girl again and never marry her. It wasn't her, necessarily, but it was that feeling of being connected to another person that he craved. If only he could find a woman and have that same feeling again. He'd never had that with Mary Lou or anyone else. If he'd had that feeling once in his life, then maybe, just maybe, he'd find it once more.

Had *Gott* brought Hazel, with those same large green eyes as that girl, Livy, and put her right there in front of him to remind him to wait for a woman he'd connect with on that level?

He thought about the similarity of that girl and Hazel. Although Hazel looked very much the same, it couldn't have been Hazel because she lived in a different community than the one he'd visited, and besides that, her name was different. He shrugged, imagining that girl now grown up with five children and never having given his proposal of marriage that day in the woods another thought.

When he woke up in the morning, he recalled that he'd dreamed that Mary Lou got married to someone else and he met Livy again at the wedding. Livy and he fell in love for real and were married. In his dream, Hazel had played the part of Livy. It would be hard to see her at work after having had a dream like that.

~

ON SATURDAY MORNING, Aunt Bee collected Hazel from the bus station. They'd already greeted each other with hugs, and were in the buggy headed to Bee's *haus*.

"She's at my place."

"Really? They let her out?"

"*Jah*. She's been doing fine on the medication, so far."

"*Gut*. I'm so glad. You can call me at the bishop's *haus* and give me updates on her, you know."

"I don't like to disturb them."

"They wouldn't mind, and it would be reassuring to me." She was glad to be home on familiar ground. It had been stressful dealing with new people and getting used to living in a new place. Although Ruth and John had been unfailingly kind, she was always careful that she didn't do anything to annoy them.

"How's the new job?"

"It's going fine and everyone is so nice, and I've met

a friend who's invited me out with her friends. Well, she said she'd arrange something."

"I'm so happy about that. That's just what you need, to mix with young people and forget all your troubles."

"It's hard when all I can think about is *Mamm* and hoping she's okay."

"You leave the worrying to me."

"*Denke*, Aunt Bee. I really don't know what I would've done without you."

"*Gott* is the one we need to thank. He's the one who's in control, not us."

"*Jah*, I forget that sometimes. If I would just remember that, I wouldn't need to worry so much. How is *Mamm*? Does she have any idea of what's going on, or is she still in another space?"

"She's back with us. She knows what's real and what's not. She's been doing a lot of crying, but the doctor said that's not a bad thing, that it might help her heal. She'll be so pleased to see you."

THEY PULLED up at Aunt Bee's house and Hazel hurried inside to see her mother.

"*Mamm!*" Her mother was sitting on the couch with a blanket over her knees. She'd lost so much weight that her cheeks were sunken in and she had dark circles under her eyes. Her face brightened when she saw Hazel, and she spread her arms out. Hazel ran to the couch, knelt down, and hugged her.

"Where have you been?"

Hazel gulped as guilt rippled through her body. The medical bills were huge and Bee and her husband had offered to help pay them, but Hazel needed every cent from her job so they wouldn't carry that burden alone. She'd lost her local bookkeeping job because of all the time she'd had to take off while looking after her mother after Hazel's father had left them. Her income from the job with the Fullers was sorely needed. Hazel couldn't be in two places at once. "I've been working, *Mamm.* In Lancaster County, with a lovely family. They make kitchen cabinets."

"Where's our *haus?* Why am I here with Bee?"

Disappointment filled Hazel's heart and she steeled herself not to cry. It didn't seem like her mother had improved much at all. "We couldn't continue paying the rent on the *haus, Mamm,* and that's why we came to live with Bee. Isn't that exciting? You like Bee, she's your favorite *schweschder.*" That almost always made her mother chuckle, as Bee was also her only sister.

Instead of laughing now, her mother stared at her with her bottom lip quivering just slightly.

"How are you?" Hazel asked, trying not to look worried.

"I'm fine." Then her mother began to cry.

Hazel figured she was crying about her husband,

Hazel's father, who'd left them. He was the only reason her mother cried. "We'll be fine, *Mamm*. I'm working to get us money and one day we'll have a nice place of our own again. It'll be just like the old days, only better." Better because her father wouldn't be able to cause them any more pain. He was finally out of their lives for good.

Bee walked in the door with Hazel's overnight bag. "*Ach, denke,* Aunt Bee. I clean forgot to get my bag. I was so excited to see *Mamm.*"

"That's fine. I'll put it up in your room. You stay talking to your *mudder.*"

Hazel gave her an appreciative nod and turned back to her mother, who was quietly sobbing. "It's okay, *Mamm.* It's all good."

"*Nee*, it's not. Where's Doug?"

"He's gone and he's not coming back. He doesn't care about us anymore." Hazel thought the truth was best. Doug wasn't coming back and that was that.

"Where is he?"

"He left us for an *Englisch* woman."

"Why?"

Hazel shook her head. He was always coming and going, in and out of their lives ever since Hazel could remember. She'd lost respect for him long ago, but every time Doug left, he took a little piece of her mother with him. Now Hazel was looking at a shell of a woman. "We don't need him."

"I do," she said in a small voice.

"Nee, you don't. Neither of us needs him. You might think you do, but you don't."

"Why haven't I ever been good enough?"

"Mamm, it's Doug who wasn't good enough. He wasn't a right fit for us."

"He's your *vadder."*

"Well, he was never much of a *vadder.* Neither of us could rely on him." She took her mother's crumpled handkerchief from her hands, and wiped her tears away. The first time she remembered having to wipe away her mother's tears was at the age of five. Then Doug would return, only to leave again, a pattern repeated every few years. It seemed just when he'd regained her mother's trust, he'd leave again. "Forget about *Dat.* We can get by without him."

"I thought things were different this time. I thought he'd stay."

"We can't trust him or the things he says. We can't let him hurt us anymore." Hazel had never let a man get close. Seeing the relationship between her mother and father had put her off relationships. Doug had told someone he'd never had a *rumspringa* and that was the reason he was so unsettled. He was in and out of the community so much that the bishop not only had to have strong words with him, he'd been shunned three times that Hazel could remember. During that time, her mother and she weren't supposed to talk or eat with him, but that was difficult, nearly impossible when he ruled the household and had a violent temper.

"Are you staying here now, Hazel?"

"Only for tonight and I must leave tomorrow afternoon. I'm staying at Ruth and John's house. John is the bishop in the community where I'm staying in Lancaster County. They're lovely people and they've made me welcome."

Her mother took hold of her hand. "Can't you stay?"

She looked into her mother's eyes. She couldn't stay because she needed the money to cover all their expenses. Since her father left they had fallen into bad debt. "I'll come back every weekend. You'll have Bee here."

Bee walked back into the room. "That's right, Judy. We've been having a good time, you and I, haven't we?"

Her mother nodded. "It's been good. We've been sewing a bit."

"That's great, *Mamm*. You love sewing."

Her mother turned to Hazel. "Have you heard from your *vadder* at all?"

"*Nee, Mamm,* and I don't expect to. We've got to let him go. He's out of our lives for good."

"I have letters to give you that I've written him. Won't you send them to him?"

"I don't know where he is."

"When you find out where he is you can send them to him."

Hazel nodded. "Okay. I'll take them with me when I leave tomorrow." Hazel had no intention of sending those letters, and neither had she any intention of trying to find out where her father was. There was no point. But she didn't want to set her mother's treatment back by telling her so. Hazel was just glad *Mamm* was now out of the hospital, but she didn't know if her mother would ever fully recover from all the mental abuse heaped on her by Doug over the past years. He had always put her down and told her she was no good and couldn't do anything right.

He'd also told her on many occasions that no one else had wanted to marry her and she was lucky to have him. Hazel could only listen to the nasty things her father said to her mother. Doug rarely spoke to her and if Hazel spoke to him, she rarely got more than a grunt in return.

Every time Doug was getting ready to walk out on them, as a cruel parting jab, he'd tell Judy he would've stayed if she'd been able to give him more children. She in turn was always blaming his bad behavior on herself. Hazel remembered hearing her mother say, *If only I'd been a better wife and given him more kinner, then he would've stayed.* Even as a child, Hazel had known he was lying and she had seen right through him. He never paid her any attention, so why would he have wanted more children? They were cruel words said simply to make Judy feel inadequate and worthless as a woman. The worst thing for her mother would be if he were to come back.

The last time he left, Hazel could tell it was the last of the last. He'd found himself an *Englisch* woman at his workplace and had left to move in with her, after taking all their rent money and all their savings. There was no coming back from that.

"Why don't you and Hazel take a walk in the sunshine?" Bee suggested to Judy.

"*Jah*, let's, *Mamm*."

"Okay."

Hazel stood and then held out her hands and helped her mother to her feet.

Once they were outside walking along the fence line of Bee's property, her mother said, "I hope one day I can be a better *mudder* to you."

"You're the best *mudder*. What are you talking about?"

"I'm not. I've tried, but I've been sad most of the time and that can't have been good for you to be around."

"I'm fine. I've turned out okay, haven't I?"

"*Jah*, but no thanks to me."

"Stop talking like that, *Mamm*."

"I hope you have a better life than I've had. Be careful who you marry. That's one piece of advice I can pass on to you."

"I will. That's for certain." Marriage was nice to

dream about, and if she ever found the perfect man she might marry. But she'd always been fearful any man might turn out like her father had.

"There are nice men around, just be sure that you marry one of them. Don't fall in love with someone who'll break your heart."

Hazel nodded, but didn't ask her mother how to tell which was which. Her mother hadn't known what Doug was like until after they married. She didn't dare ask how to be sure in case it raised bad memories, or good memories of the brief times when things had been good between them. Their relationship had been a rollercoaster of emotions, with extreme highs followed by lows that were just as intense.

HER STAY at Aunt Bee's was far too brief and Monday morning had come far too quickly.

"I was hoping to see you at the meeting yesterday, Hazel."

Hazel looked up to see Joshua. "Good morning."

"Good morning."

"I wasn't there because I went to see my family."

"In Allentown?"

"*Jah.*"

"Aren't there any jobs where your family is?"

Hazel stared at him, not knowing what to say. Fortunately, Mr. Fuller came to her rescue. "Don't bother Hazel now. She's got a lot of work to get through today."

"Sorry, Hazel."

Hazel gave a smile and a little nod and Joshua walked away. She turned back to her computer and started working again. Now she was sure that Mr. Fuller knew about her situation. The bishop must've mentioned it to him.

"Hazel, my wife would like you to come to dinner tomorrow night if you can make it. You can come home with us and then we'll take you home when it's finished, later in the evening."

"That's very kind of Mrs. Fuller. Please tell her I'd love to come for dinner."

"I will." He stepped a little closer. "How's everyone treating you here?"

"Wonderfully well. Everybody has been polite and lovely."

"Good. If that changes at any time, just come and see me."

She gave a little giggle. *"Denke,* I will."

WHEN LUNCHTIME CAME, Hazel pulled her sandwich out of her bag and the letters that her mother had forced her to take fell on the floor. She'd forgotten that she had tucked them into the bag when she packed her things for the bus trip. Hazel picked them up and put them on her desk. She knew she wasn't going to send them, and Aunt Bee had wholeheartedly agreed that she shouldn't. She only hoped her mother would be in a better state next time she went back to Bee's house. She didn't want to lie to her about sending the letters, but she also had no intention of trying to find Doug's address. She couldn't pretend to her mother that she'd sent them. It was a difficult situation to be in. Someday, she hoped, *Mamm* could be told the truth. Just when she was halfway through her sandwich and wondering how to tackle telling her mother about the letters, Isaac walked in the door.

"Hi, Hazel. Have the Williamsons called this morning?"

"Nee. The phones have been very quiet today."

"I'm just heading down to the café to get some lunch, and I just wanted to check first if there'd been any calls." He glanced over at the letters and tried to read what was on the front of them. Hazel pulled them away from him.

"Oh, I'm sorry, Hazel. I thought they were letters to do with work."

"Nee, they're my private letters."

"Oh, I'm very sorry."

"There's no need to be sorry. I had them in my bag and they fell out when I pulled out my lunch." She pushed them back into her bag. Now she was totally embarrassed about making a big fuss about the letters;

it was a weird scene. "Your *mudder* has kindly invited me for dinner tomorrow night."

"All you need is to see all of us some more." He chuckled. "Are you sure you want to?"

"*Jah.* I do. Seeing all of you boys, I'd like to meet your *mudder.* Will you be there?"

"I will."

His mother hadn't mentioned she was going to invite Hazel to dinner. Isaac hadn't been invited, but he was going to make sure he was there. Mary Lou was right, Hazel was hiding something. What had brought her so far away from her family? He was curious to know more about her and then it occurred to him that with her unusual coloring, maybe that girl he met years ago was a relative of hers. If he got the chance, he'd ask her if she had any relatives living near Falls Creek.

He'd seen the name 'Douglas' on one letter. Perhaps she had a boyfriend.

CHAPTER 8

*A*s soon as Isaac walked into the house and saw Lucy at his parents' house for dinner, he knew he'd made a huge mistake. Huge! Lucy was Levi's girlfriend and a close friend to Mary Lou. And she would tell Mary Lou, and Mary Lou would wonder why she hadn't been invited to the dinner. And *that* would give Mary Lou another reason to be displeased with him. He should have stayed at his *haus*.

He couldn't see Hazel anywhere, but his brothers were all in the living room and so was his father. He stuck his head around the kitchen doorway and saw his mother and Hazel in deep conversation. After a moment, they both looked over at him.

"Hello. I was just seeing where you were, Hazel. I didn't see you out with the others."

"Hazel and I were just talking. She offered to help

me with the dinner, but I told her it was already done. There's nothing more to do and the tables are set. All we have to do now is make the gravy."

"I'll leave you to it then." He walked into the living room and joined the others.

His father looked over at him. "Where's Mary Lou?"

He wished his father hadn't said that in front of everyone. "I only came at the last minute and I'm not sure why I didn't invite her." He wasn't looking forward to having a very difficult conversation with Mary Lou the next time he saw her. As it was now, Lucy hadn't even looked at him. She was obviously disgusted with him and sorry for her good friend.

Throughout dinner, Isaac noticed that whenever anyone asked Hazel a personal question, either his mother or his father found a way to deflect it. They were protecting her secret. He was certain she was running away from something. Whatever it was, he was sure it was something where she wasn't to blame, otherwise she wouldn't have been staying at the bishop's house.

It was hard to get to know Hazel better because she revealed nothing about her life other than the fact that she was an only child and had been raised in a small community near Allentown.

After dinner, everyone gathered in the living room for coffee. Just when there was a lull in the conversation, their overly-fat tabby cat, Tibbles, walked into the living room.

"Oh, what a beautiful cat!"

"This is Tibbles," Mrs. Fuller said.

Tibbles looked directly at Hazel as if he knew what she had said. His tail lifted straight into the air and he held his head high as he set his green eyes onto Hazel's green eyes. As much as a fat cat can slink, he slunk toward Hazel and smoothed himself against her legs.

Everyone laughed.

"You've found a friend," Benjamin said.

"He likes you," Joshua added.

Hazel stroked his back. "I love cats."

"Do you have any pets at home?" Isaac asked.

"Nee, my *vadder* would never allow me to have a pet. He said they were a waste of time and money."

"That's awful," Lucy said. "Childhood years should be filled with animals, with puppies and kittens and baby chickens. I had a pet piglet."

"I've always wanted a cat," Hazel said, still smoothing the fat cat's fur.

"You can have Tibbles," Mr. Fuller said jokingly.

"I would love to take him, but I don't know what Bishop John and Ruth would say about that."

Everyone laughed again and then Tibbles jumped up on her lap unexpectedly and started rubbing himself on her neck.

"Get down, Tibbles," Isaac said.

"*Nee*, he's fine."

"He knows you like him," Mrs. Fuller said.

Hazel giggled. "He's just lovely, although a little heavy. I don't think I've ever seen a cat as large."

"Push him off if he's bothering you," Joshua said.

"*Nee*, he's fine. He's lovely."

THAT NIGHT, Isaac had seen a different side of Hazel. Even though he knew no history of her, he guessed that she'd been raised by a strict man, just going by what she'd said. What father could deny an only child a pet? It wasn't as though they would've lived in a small apartment. They'd lived in an Amish community and that meant with plenty of land.

It had melted Isaac's heart when he'd seen how gentle and loving Hazel had been with Tibbles. He knew he was thinking about Hazel far too much lately, and that it was way more than he'd been thinking about Mary Lou.

∼

ANOTHER WEEK CAME AND WENT, and now Hazel was back at Aunt Bee's house.

"The real reason I wanted you to move away and take that job is I think you need a normal life for a while. For the next two weekends, I want you to stay there, make some friends. You've spent your whole life living in your mother's shadow and being her helper, and it's been that way for far too long. You need to get a life for yourself. That's what your *mudder* wants for you more than anything."

Hazel gulped. She knew that her mother wanted her by her side. "Did *Mamm* say that?"

"We both know that your *mudder* isn't in her right mind at the moment. But if she was in her right mind, that's what she'd want."

"If I don't come back next weekend, she'll think I've abandoned her just like Doug kept doing. She's only got me."

"Nee, she won't. You leave her to me. We'll both talk to her tonight."

"I can't see how she'll agree to it. I feel bad enough being gone through the week."

"At some point, you have to think about yourself and your life. You can't let what your *vadder* did ruin your life."

"But I'm not."

"You've got to realize that your *mudder* might not recover from this for a few years, Hazel, and how old will you be then?"

"I don't know."

"How old are you now?"

"Twenty-six."

"You might be a lot older when she finally gets her

head together. And who knows? She might never come right. You're so young, and you deserve to live a good life."

Hazel shook her head. "I've got to be there for her. I've always been there for her and nothing will change that. I don't care what happens to me. *Mamm* and I are a team, we've always been like that."

"I understand what you're saying, but I'm worried about you. You should be off doing fun things with people your own age."

"I don't care about any of that. I just want my *mudder* to be okay. She is the most important person in my life. We've only got each other." Then Hazel thought through her words. "And we've got you and *Onkel* Luke. If it weren't for you two, we'd be in a mess."

"*Jah*, you would." Aunt Bee sighed. "As you said, you've both got me and *Onkel* Luke. Don't forget that."

"I won't. We would probably be living on the street if it weren't for the both of you."

"That's a bit of an exaggeration. You'd never be on the street."

"You know what I mean. We would've been living with someone else in the community, I guess, and I know *Mamm* wouldn't like that."

"I am going to have a talk with her about you not coming home next weekend."

Hazel opened her mouth to speak and then Aunt

Bee said, "Just let me talk to her. She's getting stronger every day. You can't make friends if you're not there on the weekends."

"You can talk to her and see what she says, but I want to be here every weekend."

"You've got to think what's best for your life."

Hazel shrugged. "To keep you happy, if *Mamm* says she doesn't mind, and if I believe she truly doesn't mind, I will stay in Lancaster County next weekend."

"Good girl. Let's see how it goes, shall we?"

Hazel nodded. "Okay."

LATER, when they brought up the subject of next weekend to Hazel's mother, Hazel could see the worry in her mother's face.

"I've been troubled about that and I'm glad you brought it up with me, Bee. Hazel, you should settle somewhere and make a life for yourself without me. You probably should've done that a long time ago. We've been too close."

"I'm working so we can have a life together, *Mamm*."

"Forget about me. It's you I'm concerned about."

"Me?"

"*Jah,* you. It doesn't matter what happens to me. I don't care about myself anymore. I just care about you, and you deserve a good life."

"We'll both have a good life. You're still young, *Mamm.* You're speaking as though your life is over."

"I'm nearly fifty."

"Fifty is considered young these days. Haven't you heard that life begins at fifty?"

Her mother shook her head. *"Nee,* but I suppose you're right. Maybe we can both have a new life."

"That's right, we *can* have a new life."

Bee said, "I think it's important for Hazel to make some friends where she is."

"I have made some friends. The bishop and his wife have been lovely and the people I work with are very nice. They're the Fullers and they had me over for dinner the other night. It was so nice. They have a large fat cat, and I wanted to take him home."

"But aren't they all boys, Hazel?" Bee asked.

"Jah, the Fullers have all boys, but the two older ones have girlfriends and I've gotten to know them."

"That sounds very sociable," her mother said.

"I'm mixing with a lot of people for being there just a short amount of time."

"You need to be meeting women your age, and of course—"

Hazel interrupted her aunt. "Don't say a man. I'm not ready to be married yet."

"Nee, I'm not saying you have to get married right away, but it wouldn't hurt you to meet a nice young man and then just see what happens."

"Are any of the men at work or any of the Fuller boys suitable?" her mother asked, sounding half rational for the first time.

"Nee, none of them. Like I said, the oldest two have girlfriends and the rest are too young."

"Your aunt is right. Stay there just this weekend and I'll see you the weekend after."

"Are you sure, *Mamm?* I don't even want to stay there for the weekend. I want to come back and see you."

Her mother smiled and nodded. "Just this weekend and see what friends you can make."

"Okay, if that's what you both want."

"That would make me happy," her mother said.

Hazel was convinced it was too early for her mother to go so long without seeing her. She had to trust that Bee knew what she was doing. Bee had also been through the dreadful ups and downs of their life with Doug, watching from the sidelines.

CHAPTER 9

Isaac had just collected Mary Lou for their usual Monday night meal at the diner.

"I've been upset," she said with a pout.

He'd known there was something wrong with her the moment she'd stepped up into the buggy. He gripped the reins and glanced over at her. "What about?"

"You didn't invite me to dinner with Hazel. You want me to be friends with Hazel, so why didn't you include me in dinner at your parents' house? You always take me there for dinner, so why didn't you the other night? I could tell Lucy was acting funny and then she told me she was there the other night and I wasn't."

He knew she must've just heard about the dinner

from Lucy that morning, as she'd mentioned nothing about it over the weekend. He could see in the dim moonlight that she was pouting and had her arms folded over her chest.

There was no right answer. The truth was he'd forgotten, but he didn't think it would go over well for Mary Lou to know that. He took a deep breath. "Forgive me, Mary Lou. I've had a lot on my mind lately. I meant to invite you, but I only found out about the dinner shortly before it was on. It was no big deal. Just a dinner with Hazel to make her feel more at home."

"What have you had going on? There doesn't seem to be anything more than usual. I can't see how you could just forget to invite me. You could've come and gotten me."

"You know my job has certain stresses."

"I don't see why. You don't even run the business. Your *vadder* does. How stressed will you be when you take over? You need to learn to live with the stress."

"My *vadder* and I don't see eye-to-eye on a lot of things. When I'm running things, I won't have that issue."

"That's not what I'm talking about. It seems you completely forgot that I was in your life and it makes me wonder why. And you not getting along with your *vadder* has got nothing to do with why I wasn't invited the other night."

"All I can say is that I'm sorry."

"I will accept your apology. I'm not happy about it, though. It makes me wonder how important I am to you."

"You're very important to me; it's just that I'm stupid sometimes."

"You said it, not me."

She was starting to relax, he noticed. "It wasn't a big deal. My *mudder* just wanted to make Hazel feel more comfortable."

"Did you find out anything about Hazel's secret from your *vadder?*"

"*Nee*, I didn't, but I think you're right that she's keeping something from people. Whatever it is, it's none of our business."

"I was right. I knew there was something wrong with her."

"I don't think there's anything wrong with her. She just seems to have something going on in her life that she wants to keep to herself. Anyway, am I forgiven?"

"As long as you don't do anything like that again."

"I won't."

She gave a little giggle. "I forgive you, then."

"Phew." He wiped imaginary sweat from his brow, which made her giggle again.

"I'm going to have Hazel over to my *haus* one time for dinner with my friends."

"She'd appreciate that, I'm sure. She seemed to enjoy the other night."

～

After a busy week at work, the next weekend came and went. Hazel had called her mother and she seemed to be doing fine. Hazel was able to relax and get to know some of Ruth and the bishop's visitors.

CHAPTER 10

The next Monday night, Isaac was driving Mary Lou home from their dinner.

"It's been a couple of weeks, so don't you think it's time we talked about the wedding?"

"I'm sure I said we'd talk about it in a few weeks time."

"Weeks, months, what's the difference?"

He chuckled, "There's a lot of difference between weeks and months. I told you I need time and I did say months." He emphasized the word 'months.' He didn't want to hurt her, but he needed time to prepare himself mentally to spend the rest of his life with another person.

"There's a lot of preparation that goes into a wedding, so I think I need to talk about it sooner rather than later."

"I hear what you're saying. We just need to have this conversation in a few weeks. Besides, I haven't asked you to marry me yet, so we shouldn't be discussing the subject at all."

She turned to him and her eyes grew wide. He knew he had made a mistake as soon as the words had carelessly tumbled out of his mouth.

"What exactly are you saying? Haven't we decided on each other?"

He had to be truthful. Otherwise, the woman would soon be running every aspect of his life. He had enough of having no power at work; surely in his personal life he was allowed some freedom of choice. "I don't want the future moment to be ruined by you forcing things on me when I'm not ready."

"Is this what you're saying to me—that you're not sure about me?"

That was the question he was not ready to answer, but now that question was staring him boldly in the face. Where was that special feeling he'd had with that girl from years ago? He'd fallen in to the habit of dating Mary Lou, without giving it too much thought, but now she and everyone else expected them to marry. Either he waited until he found that same feeling with someone, or he did the sensible and expected thing, and went ahead with the marriage to Mary Lou.

"I'm waiting for an answer." Her tone was calm and quiet.

He desperately scrambled for a few more seconds of thinking time. "What is the question?"

"Are you hesitating because you're not sure about me?"

"I'm sure that you're a lovely person and any man would want to marry you."

"We're not talking about any man, we're talking about you."

He shook his head. "If I'm truthful, I have to say that I'm just not sure; at the same time, I don't want to let you go."

Her mouth fell open in shock and tears came to her eyes. "Well, it looks like I'll have to make that decision for you."

"What do you mean?"

"It's obvious, isn't it?"

She was ending things with him. "Don't rush into anything in anger. Give it some thought."

"That's the whole problem. You're giving things way too much thought. Maybe that's it. Either way, I want a man who can't live without me, not someone who is still deciding about me after two years, or someone who is waiting for someone better to come along."

She was right. What she said made sense. He could see that, now that she had said it aloud. "You're right. It's best that we end things."

"End our relationship?"

"Isn't that what you were getting at?"

"You're just impossible. Stop the buggy."

He slowed the buggy and then stopped it on the side of the road. She jumped down.

"What are you doing?" he called out.

"I'm walking home."

"Don't be ridiculous. You can't do that at this hour of night. It's too dark."

"I'm only half a mile from home and I'm not ridiculous. You're the one who's ridiculous."

She turned and, with her hands balled into fists, she stomped ahead.

He jumped down from the buggy and ran after her. "Stop, Mary Lou!"

She spun around. "I should've known this a long time ago and we should've ended things a long time ago. Now you've wasted years of my life." She turned away from him and started walking again.

He stopped in his tracks. "They weren't wasted."

"They were," she shouted into the night. She spun back around and took a step toward him. "I'm so angry I could hit you."

"Do it if it makes you feel better."

She tipped her head up to the sky and screamed. "You're so impossible." She walked away.

"You can't walk by yourself."

She ignored him and kept walking. He hurried back to the buggy and had no choice but to follow behind her until she got to the driveway of her home.

"I'm going now since you're home," he called out to her.

Without speaking, she walked more quickly and then broke into a run. When he saw she was safely in the house, he turned the buggy around, feeling deeply disappointed in himself. At this rate, he was going to end up a bachelor forever. He felt bad for her, but at the same time he didn't know what to do. She was clearly more anxious to get married than he. He didn't want to let her go, but only because they'd been together for so long. It annoyed him that nothing felt right to him. It didn't feel right to let her go, but neither did it feel right to commit to a marriage until he was sure. The best thing he could do for Mary Lou, if she wanted to marry soon, was to let her go and hope she'd find someone who suited her better.

∽

THE NEXT MORNING AT WORK, Isaac was surprised to see Mary Lou walk into the workshop after the words they'd had the night before. He was sitting beside Hazel's desk making his usual morning phone calls and scheduling appointments.

Mary Lou ignored him and started talking to Hazel. When he hung up from his call, he waited for a lull in their conversation. "Hello, Mary Lou."

"Hello, Isaac. I'm here to see Hazel." She spoke as

though nothing was wrong between them and stepped back toward Hazel. "Anyway, Hazel, I know you're working, so I won't hold you up. I just called in quickly to say that I'm having dinner with my friends tomorrow night at my house and I'd like you to join us. I can collect you from work and also take you back to the bishop's *haus* when it's over."

"*Denke* very much. I'd like that."

A smile spread across Mary Lou's face. "Good, I can't wait."

"Me either. Can I bring something?"

"Of course not. Just bring yourself."

Isaac could only stare at Mary Lou, wondering what she was doing. Did she think that Hazel had something to do with his indecision? Hazel had only been there a short time, so that didn't quite make sense since he'd been with Mary Lou for two years. One thing he knew about Mary Lou was that she didn't do anything without a good reason. Given her current state of mind, Isaac guessed she was jealous of Hazel and thought she had something to do with their troubles.

Once Mary Lou had her answer from Hazel regarding dinner, she flounced out of the office. Hazel didn't look at Isaac who was still sitting there stunned. She just went back to tapping away at the computer keys.

CHAPTER 11

The next night, Hazel hurried out to Mary Lou's waiting buggy.

"*Denke* for this, Mary Lou. I've really been looking forward to meeting people."

"Hazel, I'm so sorry, but I've had to call the dinner off. I suppose I should've called you at work. You see, my *mudder* is sick."

"Oh, nothing serious I hope?"

"*Nee,* just a virus, I think. Anyway, I thought you and I could have a bite to eat somewhere, just the two of us."

"Yeah, I'd like that."

"*Gut.* I'll take you to the diner where Isaac and I go every Monday and Thursday night. It's a way we can spend time together alone, but not really be alone if you know what I mean."

"Jah, that sounds like a nice idea."

When they were seated in the diner, Mary Lou passed her a menu. "Isaac likes the steak sandwich. I know all his favorite foods so I'll be able to cook them all when we get married."

"Jah, and that's not far away." She looked down the list of food.

"Did he say anything to you?"

Hazel looked up at Mary Lou. "Isaac?"

"Jah, has he said anything about me lately?"

"Nee, we only talk about work."

"Oh. That sounds boring."

"Did you work today?"

"Only this morning for four hours. I work afternoons on Thursday and Monday, and then at other times when they need me. My roster changes from week to week except for those two shifts. Anyway, it brings me in some money. I've saved a lot of money and bought things for our *haus* already. I want to be a *fraa* who contributes a lot."

All the talk about marriage made Hazel a little envious. She imagined herself living in a house, a real home, with a special loving man. Then she wiped the scene from her mind, as it would most likely never happen.

"I would've thought you'd be married by your age, Hazel."

"Jah, me too." Hazel gave a little giggle. Her life

hadn't been a normal one. "I'm staying here for the weekend, so I'll be able to come to the Sunday meeting."

"Good. I'll introduce you to my friends."

"I'd like that." She looked down at the menu again, trying to choose something while Mary Lou chatted about what her life would be like when she married Isaac.

THE FOLLOWING WEEKEND, Hazel also stayed in Lancaster County just like Aunt Bee had wanted.

As she was washing up the breakfast dishes with Ruth on Saturday morning, Ruth made a suggestion. "Why don't you take one of the buggies and explore the area?"

"Denke, but I couldn't. I might get lost. I don't have a good sense of direction."

Ruth smiled at her and then emptied the sink of water. "I'd go with you, but we've got a few people visiting John today for counseling. There is a road map in the buggy under the seat."

Hazel guessed that Ruth wanted her out of the way for the day since they had people to counsel. Maybe they had people coming to the house who had marriage problems or perhaps people with monetary or farming disputes. "I could have a look around the main part of town. I know the way there."

"*Jah*, why don't you do that?"

"I will. I'm glad you suggested it. Can I bring anything back from town for you?"

"*Nee.* I think we've got everything. Whenever you're ready to go, I'll help you hitch the buggy."

By midmorning, Hazel was putting her troubles behind her while her borrowed horse trotted the buggy through the streets by the open fields. Although she missed her mother, it was good to be free of the pressure of keeping her mother's mood elevated and hoping she didn't say anything that would make her mother burst into tears.

She didn't feel she knew Mary Lou well enough to stop by her *haus* to see if she wanted to come out with her for a few hours. Besides, Mary Lou would probably be spending time with Isaac, seeing it was the weekend. Although she might've enjoyed Mary Lou's company, she didn't need to hear talk of marriage again. That was all Mary Lou had talked about the other night over their dinner.

Hazel found her way into town and parked her buggy, figuring she'd look at some small stores on foot. When she spotted a craft shop, she headed toward it. Before she got there, she noticed an Amish woman down an alleyway. Looking closer, she stopped when she realized the woman was Mary Lou. Then Hazel saw that Mary Lou was speaking with a young *Englisch* man. Something about the scene looked very wrong to Hazel. Then Mary Lou stepped forward and kissed the young man, and he kissed her back.

Hazel stood there staring, frozen to the spot, not believing what she saw. Seeming to sense someone staring at them, the young man looked up and saw her. Before Hazel could make her legs move, Mary Lou swung around and saw her. Mary Lou hurried toward her and Hazel's legs suddenly started moving.

She did not want to talk to Mary Lou. There was nothing to say.

"Stop, Hazel!"

Hazel stopped in her tracks and waited for Mary Lou to catch up.

"What you saw just now—"

"Was horrible, just horrible." It brought back memories of her father's philandering ways. Her mother had even hidden many things he did from the bishop, knowing Doug wouldn't have been allowed back in the community if his ways had been found out. There could be nothing worse for a person in a relationship than to be cheated on. Hazel felt dreadfully sorry for Isaac.

"Just forget what you saw and please don't tell anyone."

She shook her head. Secrecy never helped any situation. "I can't do that."

"You can and you must."

"What you've done destroys people, Mary Lou."

She frowned. "You're being stupid. It was just a silly mistake. I won't do it again."

Hazel turned around to see where the young man was. "Who was he?"

"Just a boy I met a while ago."

Mary Lou's response seemed very casual to Hazel.

"You don't understand," Hazel said.

"It doesn't matter to me what you think as long as you don't tell anyone."

Hazel knew that something like that had to be told. "Isaac must be told. You must confess what happened and then you should work things out with him. Things can always be worked out if they're not covered up."

Mary Lou stepped forward. "Please don't tell him. I was just upset with him about something. We had a little disagreement, it was nothing really, but it made me upset. If he finds out about this he'll be hurt and upset and he'll call off the marriage."

"I wouldn't feel right about keeping that kind of a secret. If there's a problem in your relationship, just talk about it." She couldn't tell Mary Lou that it was secrets like that that had ruined her life and her mother's life. Her father had covered up what he'd done, and sometimes her mother had covered for him too, and there was nothing worse than not knowing the truth. If her father had come to her mother and told her he wanted to leave and didn't want to be in the relationship anymore that would've saved her mother a lot of pain.

"I thought you were my friend, Hazel. I had planned to take you to my home and for you to meet all my friends."

"I am your friend, but you really need to tell him. Don't you want to be with Isaac anymore?"

"Of course I do. That kiss meant nothing and it won't happen again. It was a moment of weakness. Anyone can have a weak moment, and *Gott* will forgive me when I confess what I've done."

"It's just that it's horrible..."

"You think I'm horrible?"

"*Nee*, I don't. It's an awful situation."

"It's really none of your business, Hazel. I don't know why you're setting yourself up to be so high and mighty, like you're Little Miss Perfect. Go on, tell him for all I care." She turned and hurried away.

"Wait up, Mary Lou."

Mary Lou kept walking. Hazel didn't know what to do. In her heart, she knew the right thing to do was to tell Isaac. If someone had told her mother what Doug had been like, that would've saved years of pain, but everyone who knew had kept quiet about his philandering ways. She caught up to Mary Lou. "Wait!"

Mary Lou swung around. "What?"

"I've decided that I won't tell Isaac, but you'll have to tell him."

Mary Lou frowned and shot her a scowl before she swung away from her and walked away.

"Well?"

"Okay," she yelled over her shoulder. "I'll tell him before the weekend's out."

"If you don't, I will."

"I said I would." Mary Lou stomped away.

Hazel was pleased that at least she was walking in the other direction from the alleyway where she'd been with the *Englischer*. It was a weight off Hazel's shoulders that she didn't have to tell Isaac. They hadn't gotten off to a great start and that would've made him feel awkward with her.

CHAPTER 12

It was Saturday afternoon and Isaac decided it was time to do some much overdue housework. He took hold of the broom and began to sweep the porch. Leaves and dirt were strewn across the entire length of it. As he was just about to continue his sweeping efforts inside the house, he noticed a buggy heading toward his house. Looking harder, he recognized Mary Lou's buggy. He leaned the broom against the house and walked outside to meet her. He wondered if she was there to resurrect the relationship.

She jumped down as soon as the buggy stopped, and looked over at him.

"Is everything okay?" he asked.

"*Jah*, I just didn't like the way things were left the other day."

"Neither did I. There's no reason why we can't be friends."

"That's right, and as a friend, I thought I should warn you about something, or rather someone."

"What do you mean?"

"Hazel and I had dinner the other night. I tried to be a friend to her but it's hard. She's hiding something like we've said before. I'm not exactly sure what."

"It can't be anything too bad since the bishop has her staying at his house."

"It might be wise to keep an eye on her, have you thought about that?"

He scratched his head. He hadn't thought of that.

"Maybe she got herself into some kind of trouble and the bishop's trying to keep her on the straight and narrow."

"What has this got to do with us, though?" he asked. "She only works for me."

"I think she's in love with you and I just wanted to warn you to be careful. She seems a bit shifty to me, like she could be a dreadful liar."

He raised his eyebrows. "That seems a little harsh, to say she's a liar."

"I think she seems like one, I didn't say she was one. I'm just worried that you might be influenced by her pretty face."

"Mary Lou, you and I not being together has nothing to do with anyone else."

"I know that. That's not what I'm saying. I just don't trust her and I don't think that you should. That's all I'm saying."

"Denke. For the warning."

She looked over his shoulder at the house. "Are you doing some cleaning?"

"That's mostly what I do on a Saturday afternoon when I'm not with you."

"I miss our times together."

He nodded.

"Do you?"

"Jah, I do. But I want to be fair to you, and that's why things are the way they are. You can't wait forever and I understand that."

"You're not mad at me?" she asked.

"Me mad at you? *Nee!"*

She giggled. "I thought you might have been, for the way I walked away from you the other night."

"Never. We've spent a lot of time together. You'll always hold a special place in my heart."

"That's good to know."

"How about I get us a cold drink of lemonade? We can sit on the porch and drink it."

"You made it yourself?"

"Nee, Mamm made it. Come on, it'll get me out of doing my chores for a while."

She giggled. "Okay, but just for a moment."

All throughout Monday morning, Hazel was sick with nerves. She couldn't tell from Isaac's face if his girlfriend had told him what had happened. When lunchtime came, instead of having lunch in the office, she walked to a payphone down the road near the shops. She called Mary Lou's number and was grateful that Mary Lou answered and not another member of her family.

"Mary Lou?"

"Who's this?"

"It's Hazel.

"Hello, Hazel." Her voice was cold and Hazel knew she wasn't ever going to get that dinner invitation to Mary Lou's house.

"I'm just wondering if you've told him yet."

"Told who what?"

This wasn't going the way she'd planned. "Told Isaac about that *Englischer?*"

"I thought about it and I'm not going to tell him."

This was what Hazel had feared. She didn't want to be the one to have to tell Isaac, but now she had to. "You said you would."

"I changed my mind."

"I said I'd tell him if you didn't."

Mary Lou gave a large sigh. "Do what you have to do. And if you tell him, you could lose your job."

"How could I, if I'm only telling him the truth? If he finds out later it could hurt him more."

"Okay, okay. I'll tell him, just give me some more time. Give me another day or two. This isn't easy, you know."

"You'll really tell him?"

"Jah, but just realize he might not want to know the truth. Some people are happy in their ignorance."

"Telling him is the best thing to do."

Mary Lou grunted, "Goodbye," and hung up the phone.

CHAPTER 13

A few days later, Mr. Fuller came into her office reading a letter and looking worried.

"You don't look very happy, Mr. Fuller."

He looked up at her from under his bushy eyebrows. "I'm not. We've just got a letter from the IRS. We're being audited, it seems."

"Oh, they had an audit in the last place I worked. It wasn't good."

"What happened?"

"Everything worked out in the end. It's just that they go through everything—all the records, and they have to be in order."

"The books are all right, aren't they?"

No, they weren't, but she didn't want to let him know that Isaac wasn't a brilliant bookkeeper. She avoided telling him, as best she could. "They go back over the last few years. And I don't know if they'll be able to understand the previous accounting system before it went onto the computer."

"Can you take a look at it?"

"Of course I will. I'll need Isaac's help because he'll need to tell me why he did certain things so that I can understand how he used to do things. Can I have a look at the letter?" He handed it to her and she read it. "This isn't so bad. They're saying there's a discrepancy and we just have to check it." She gave the letter back.

He lowered his head. "So, I'm taking it that Isaac made mistakes?"

She giggled to cover her nervousness. *"Nee,* not really, he just did things a little different from the way I would do them, but they weren't necessarily mistakes. I'll go over everything and take a second look."

"I hope not, because if he made any errors, it could be very costly for us."

"I'll get right on it."

Mr. Fuller looked up when Isaac came into his office. Mr. Fuller passed him the letter. Isaac took it and read it, and then looked at Hazel.

"It seems like *Gott* sent you to us at the very right time."

She pulled a face. "I hope so. I just need you to show me what you did in the old system you used before you put it onto the computer. That might help me understand a few things."

"I can do that, as long as I remember what I did. I just have a few instructions to give the boys and I'll be right back. I've got the card system I used boxed up in the back room. I'll fetch it."

"Okay."

Mr. Fuller left them to it, and when Isaac came back he had a few boxes of cards and a large ledger.

They took the next few hours to go over things.

Hazel noticed some mistakes right away. "See here? This belongs in that column, and that one should've been here."

"That's a dreadful mistake to make."

"I'll have to go through all the records. You never used an accountant?"

"We never saw the need."

"A good accountant can save you money."

"I've read up on the tax deductions and things like that and so has my *vadder*."

"They change things all the time. Every year they change things, sometimes just slightly. It's a full-time job keeping up with such things. That's why you should get an accountant to do the taxes."

"Now that the business is getting bigger, I suppose we can't keep doing things the way we used to do things when there were only three workers here."

Hazel nodded.

"How long is it going to take you to straighten out my mess?"

"It's not exactly a mess, but I'll have to go through and check everything to make sure there aren't any simple errors like this one. It's hard to say how many hours it's going to take."

He put his hands on his head. "Could you stay for an extra hour every night until this is sorted? You'll be paid for the overtime, and I'll drive you home instead of Ruth coming to get you."

"I'd be happy to do that, but I couldn't take any extra money."

"We couldn't have you working for nothing. We'll pay you for the overtime and any extra rates that the extra time might incur. Isn't the usual rate for overtime half-again your hourly wage? And since you'll soon be doing the pay checks, you'll be able to work out exactly what that is."

"Am I to be doing the payroll as well?"

"Jah, it'll save me doing it. I'm getting used to having you around." He gave her a huge smile which made her heart pitter-patter.

Mary Lou was blessed to have a man like him. If she could find a man like Isaac, someone big and strong who admitted his mistakes and set about to rectify them, she'd feel safe with a man like that.

"Denke for putting your trust in me."

"I appreciate how hard you've been working and you've been doing a great job. How about we start adding the extra hour tomorrow night?"

"Okay. I'll let Ruth know she needn't collect me."

A WEEK WENT BY. Hazel had become convinced that Mary Lou still hadn't told Isaac what had happened, and it was causing her concern. She didn't want Isaac to be in the dark about something, like her mother had been for so long. She wouldn't keep quiet. When there was no one in the office, she used the phone to call Mary Lou's home. After hanging on for a long time, the phone was eventually answered.

"Hello?"

"Mary Lou, it's Hazel."

"Oh."

"Have you told Isaac yet?"

"I wish you'd keep out of things. You're really annoying me. I thought we could've been friends."

She hadn't told him. Hazel felt sick to the stomach knowing that she was going to have to be the one to do it. When she had just ended the call, Isaac came back into the workshop and sat behind his father's computer.

Summoning all the courage she could, she decided to tell him. Although at work wasn't the ideal time, she didn't know when would be the correct time. There wasn't any good time for such news. At least his brothers were at lunch. She got up from her chair and headed into the other office.

"Can I have a word with you?"

He looked up at her and smiled. *"Jah,* of course, sit down. I was just checking on some emails."

Isaac noticed Hazel was greatly disturbed about something.

"Sit here." He jumped up and pulled a chair up to the desk. He sat back down on his father's chair. At that moment, he wondered if she was going to say she could no longer continue with the job. He regretted being so short with her when he first found her sitting in his office. If she left, he only had himself to blame.

"What is it, Hazel?"

"It's something ... something of a personal nature."

"To do with me?"

"Jah."

He had no idea what it could be. Was she going to tell him she didn't appreciate his rudeness, or had one of his brothers crossed the line with her in some way? "Tell me."

"It's a little embarrassing to talk about."

"I'll try not to blush." He smiled, trying to make light of the moment.

"I'll just come straight out and say it. I saw your girlfriend kissing an *Englischer.*"

"Mary Lou?"

"Jah."

He stared into her green eyes. She wouldn't have known that they had broken up. He was shocked to learn that about Mary Lou. As far as he knew, Mary Lou had told no one about ending their relationship, and neither had he.

"I didn't want to be the one to tell you, but things like this—secrets like this have affected my life very badly, and I wouldn't want that to happen to you."

He looked down at the desk in front of him. Hazel was a strange one. Was it true? He couldn't imagine Mary Lou doing anything of the kind. Maybe Hazel liked him and was trying to drive a wedge between him and Mary Lou.

He stood up. *"Denke* for telling me, Hazel. You should get back to work. Or you're probably still on your lunch hour."

She stood as well. "I only get half an hour for lunch."

"Okay."

"You don't believe me?"

He stared at her, wondering what to say. "The truth is, I don't know what to believe."

"I understand."

She walked out of the office and sat behind her desk.

A few minutes later, curiosity got the better of him. He stormed into her office. "Why would you tell me something as outrageous as that?"

"Because it's true. I have no reason to make up anything like that."

"Don't you?" She did if she liked him, as Mary Lou had said.

"Nee, no reason in the world."

He stared into her face. He couldn't call her a liar; all he could do was turn and walk away before he said something he would regret.

HAZEL SLUMPED BACK in her chair. She had known there was a chance he might take it badly and he had, but at least the truth was out. Now she had to deal with his awkwardness and the fact that she'd lost a friend in Mary Lou. And it could cost her this job. She sighed deeply. Things in this community weren't working out any better than back at home.

AFTER HAZEL HAD GONE home that evening, Isaac's second youngest brother, the eighteen-year-old Timothy, approached him. "I've got something to tell you and you mightn't like it."

He looked up from his father's office chair to see Timothy leaning against the doorframe. "What is it?"

"It's about Mary Lou."

Isaac frowned. "Sit down."

Timothy sat on the same chair Hazel had used

earlier. "Someone told me they saw her in an *Englischer's* car."

"A man?"

"*Jah*, he had short-cropped brown hair."

Isaac shook his head. "I don't want to know what he looked like."

"I'm sorry. I didn't want to tell you—"

"You're not the first one to mention it to me. The thing is, Mary Lou and I are no longer together."

"Really?"

"*Jah.*"

Timothy leaned forward. "Why didn't you say anything?"

"I just didn't want to. I just wanted things to settle and then people would find out in time."

"I'm sorry. That must be hard for you."

He nodded, realizing Timothy assumed that Mary Lou had broken up with him. He let him think that. "Anyway, *denke* for letting me know, Timothy."

"It wasn't easy. I thought you mightn't believe me. I thought you mightn't believe me and you'd bite my head off."

He froze when he realized he hadn't believed Hazel. If it'd been hard for Timothy to tell him, it must've been doubly hard for Hazel to do so. *She must feel dreadful.* "Did she ... Did Mary Lou ... Was it more than taking a car ride with the man?"

"Sorry, Isaac, but I was told she was sitting too close for him to be just driving her somewhere."

Isaac nodded. He had to find Hazel and apologize for not believing her. *"Denke."*

When Timothy walked away, Isaac noticed Hazel coming back into the office. He hurried over to see her. "I thought you'd gone home."

"I was leaving, but I forgot my lunch bag and all my other things. Ruth's out there waiting for me. I need to tell you I'm leaving. Tell your *vadder* I'm sorry, but this can't work out. The accounts are in order now and I've noted everything to show the IRS. We were wrong and we owe them a small amount of money. Or rather your company owes a small amount of money. It should be fine if you pay it and show them the—"

"Hazel, I'm sorry. Very sorry. I should've believed you. Don't leave on my account."

She shook her head and when he looked closer he saw her eyes were red and she'd been crying.

Her voice croaked and she could barely speak. "It's my *mudder*. I've just gotten news from Ruth that she's very sick."

"Go, then, and come back. Your job will still be here. You don't have to leave forever. Once your *mudder's* better, come back."

"You don't see. How could you? My *mudder* has just tried to kill herself."

His jaw dropped open. "What?"

"Kill herself. She's been unstable ever since my *vadder* left the first time. He left us every few years, and my *mudder* couldn't take any more sadness. *Mamm* was in an institution and now she'll have to go back and stay there for longer. It was a big mistake, me staying here for those two weekends. She thought I'd abandoned her." Tears streamed down her face. "She feels that I have abandoned her and I haven't. It's my fault."

"Hazel, that's dreadful. I mean that she'd be so low to consider something like that."

"I know." Her bottom lip trembled as she took a deep breath.

He reached out and touched her shoulder in an effort to comfort her. "Is there anything I can do? Can I take you somewhere?"

"Ruth has packed my things and she's taking me to the bus station."

"Is there anything I can do?"

"*Nee, denke.* I can't think of anything."

"Where is your *vadder* at a time like this?"

"I don't know and I don't care. He was always leaving us. Now he's living with an *Englisch* woman."

"I'm so sorry. If it helps in any way, this job will always be available to you if you ever want to return."

She shook her head. "It's not about what I want, but *denke*. I could never come back. I don't think I could have another job again. I'll just have to look after my *mudder* forever, for however long it takes her to get better. You see, we've only got each other." She grabbed her lunch bag. "I have to go."

He walked out of the building with her. He had to ask her something now, if there was a chance he was never going to see her again. "Hazel, I have a quick question. Did you ever live in Falls Creek?"

"Nee, but I used to go to my aunt's for holidays. She used to live near Falls Creek some years ago."

"Do you know a woman there called Livy?"

She stared at him with those large green eyes. "Did you say 'Livy'?"

"Jah."

"That was my nickname. Everyone called me Livy when I was younger."

"It's you! Do you remember a young man who proposed to you?"

Her mouth fell open. "That was you?"

A glimmer of the old feeling came back when they locked eyes. "It was me, and you agreed to marry me."

She put her hand over her mouth. "I'd completely forgotten until you mentioned it just now. You've grown a lot since then."

They were interrupted by Ruth. "Come on, Hazel, if we're to make that bus."

Isaac looked at Ruth then turned back to Hazel. "I'm sorry I didn't believe you about—"

"Isaac, believe me, that's the least of my problems

right now. It doesn't matter to me. I feel dreadful for leaving you all with no bookkeeper."

"I'll have to give that old lady her job back."

She smiled as he walked with her to the buggy. "I didn't call her old, but do tell her to be careful of what she does and to double check her work." A smile twigged at the corners of her lips. "Goodbye, Isaac."

"Goodbye, Hazel. I hope you'll be back. I don't want this to be the end."

She turned around before she got into the buggy and now frown lines marred her forehead. "I can't come back."

"I'll tell my *vadder* you've gone."

She stepped into the buggy. *"Denke.* I'll call him and explain when I get to Aunt Bee's." Hazel said a couple of words to Ruth and then looked back at Isaac. "Bye."

"Bye." Isaac stood and stared as the buggy horse clip-clopped away.

He wanted to do something about her mother. The circumstances were tragic and he felt helpless. On the side of the street, he sent up a silent prayer for God to have his hand on Hazel and her mother. The best thing he could do was keep them in his prayers.

Now the buggy was out of sight, and he turned back to the office. She hadn't been there for long, but now it was like a light had been snuffed out. What was it about this young woman? She was attractive, but not stunningly so. Her personality was quiet and deliberate, with a calm confidence radiating through her being.

His heart went out to her for surviving such an unstable life. It couldn't have been easy to live in a home full of uncertainty. That summer day he first met Hazel returned to him. What were the chances of meeting that same girl again? Why had she come back into his life? To taunt him? Now he knew for sure and for certain that he'd done the right thing in not continuing the relationship with Mary Lou.

What was up with this name of Livy, and what did it stand for? Now, that was also going to bug him until he found the answer, but would he ever? *Jah,* he would. One way or another, he knew he had to see Hazel again. God had sent her to him once again for a reason, and he was sure she was more than just a sign to look for that feeling in his heart once more. She was the person for him. He wanted her because now he knew he'd only capture that special feeling again with her.

"D<small>ENKE</small> <small>FOR ALLOWING</small> me to stay at your *haus, Ruth.*"

"We've loved having you and we hope that you'll come back anytime. Come back when your *mudder* is better."

"I don't think she'll ever be better. She's a broken woman because of my father leaving us, over and over, and then coming back and promising us he was a changed man. She thought she was doing the right thing by taking him back all the time. He'd been shunned many times and then taken back into the community. Even still, *Mamm* kept back the full extent of things from me."

"*Gott* tells us to forgive."

"It's not an easy thing to do. I would never put myself through what she's been through. I can't believe she tried to kill herself. It's all my fault. My aunt said I should make friends and make a life for myself here, but what is a life without my *mudder* in it?" Hazel sobbed into her hands.

"Things sometimes have to get worse before they get better. Now your *mudder's* at the bottom, and there's no place to go but up."

Hazel sniffed and looked up. "Do you think so?"

"*Jah,* now she'll get the help she needs."

"From the medical profession?"

"Maybe. In addition to her faith. *Gott* works in many ways, and He can use people and doctors even if they're unbelievers."

"*Jah,* I know." Hazel took a deep breath. Ruth was saying anything she could think of to make her feel better.

CHAPTER 14

When Isaac walked into his office, as vividly as a bolt of lightning on a clear summer's day he realized he'd been set up by Mary Lou. Hazel had seen Mary Lou with the *Englischer* and Mary Lou must've known that. That's when she tried to poison his mind against Hazel. She told him Hazel liked him so he wouldn't believe her if she told him about Mary Lou's dalliance with the *Englischer*. Her evil plan had worked. He *had* doubted Hazel's word when she'd told him.

But what to do? There was no point in talking to Mary Lou about anything. He wanted nothing more to do with her. The only person to show true sense and judgment about relationships was his mother. She might be able to guide him in the right way, since she understood women.

He went directly to his parents' home and found his mother setting the table for dinner. Sitting down in the kitchen, he told his mother everything he knew about what had happened with Hazel's mother.

"I'm not really surprised about what happened. Hazel's *mudder* was seriously ill. She'd had some kind of breakdown."

"You knew all this before?"

"Hazel needed a job to pay for her *mudder's* medical bills and we gave her a job."

"*Dat* did that?"

"*Jah*, and it was a nice thing to do."

"That makes sense now. He created a job where we had none. And now we realize we do need someone to do what Hazel was doing. That was generous of you and *Dat*."

"We must pray for Hazel's *mudder*."

"Of course. I was praying on the way here."

"Hazel's been through a lot."

"It's made her strong. I can see the will and determination in her eyes," he said.

"No girl should go through what she's been through. Ruth tells me she practically had to raise herself and play nursemaid to her *mudder*."

He breathed heavily. "At what point does a person get to where they … I wonder if I have a chance."

His mother looked up. "A chance of what? She's not a well woman from what I've heard."

"I feel sorry for Hazel. She's such a young girl to have all this on her shoulders. Did you hear about her *vadder?*" he asked.

"Only that he left them and he'd done it many times before."

"I'd like to be able to do something." What he'd like to be able to do was marry Hazel and give her the life she deserved. A good life with a happy home.

"What else can we do? It's not easy with her being all the way in Allentown now."

"Jah, I know. I might visit and see if there's any way I can help out. I have some money if they need that."

His mother stopped and looked up again. "Isaac, are you telling me you've got feelings for Hazel other than of friendship?"

"Jah, Mamm. I've developed feelings for her. Feelings that I never had for Mary Lou."

A smile brightened his mother's face. "What about Mary Lou?"

"I forgot to mention we're no longer together."

"That is a shock, but you feel what you feel. And if you like Hazel better, then you must do all you can to marry her."

"Marry her?"

"Jah, I won't have you engaged to another girl for two years."

He gulped, feeling guilty about Mary Lou. "I feel bad about that, *Mamm.* You didn't need to mention it."

"The facts are the facts."

"The facts are that if Hazel agreed to marry me, I would happily marry her right away."

A smile brightened his mother's face. "Well, you must tell her how you feel."

He looked down at the wood grain in the table. It was bad timing. Hazel would never leave her mother.

"Why are you looking so glum?" she asked.

"It seems I'm in a bad situation. With her *mudder's* fragile state of mind, she'd never leave her *mudder* just for her own happiness."

"Then you must wait until the *mudder* is better."

He breathed out heavily. "How long will it take?"

"I don't know, but the most important thing is, does Hazel feel the same about you?"

He looked down at the table again, rubbing his fingers over the ingrained marks on the table. He'd made his share of them as a child, with the end of a pencil. "I don't know, *Mamm*. I can only hope so."

"You never told her how you feel?"

He shook his head. *"Nee.* I couldn't, not when things had just ended with Mary Lou."

"You have to regard Mary Lou's feelings in all of this."

"I know and I'm just glad that Mary Lou and I ended things."

"You should've done it a long time ago if the feelings weren't there."

He didn't like to be reminded. His mother was good at reminding him of his failures. "*Jah*, well, I know that now."

"Do you have Hazel's phone number?" his mother asked.

"We have her Aunt Bee's phone number on file in the office."

"That could be a starting point. Call her and ask how her *mudder* is."

"*Jah*, I will."

"I'm glad you like Hazel. She's a lovely girl and she suits you just fine. She's a gentle girl and yet, as you said, she's strong. And surely her time has come to enjoy some happiness. I hope you can give that to her, Isaac."

"I will. If she gives me that chance, I will."

CHAPTER 15

At the next Sunday meeting, after the preaching was over, Isaac saw Mary Lou's mother hurrying toward him. He stopped and waited for her to approach.

"Mary Lou has left the community." Mary Lou's mother stared at Isaac as if that was all his fault.

"Really?"

"Jah, she left to be with some *Englischer*. And she said she won't be back."

"I'm sure she'll be back."

"That's not what she said."

Isaac had been there when Mary Lou had been baptized, and among the Amish, that baptism meant if she came back to the community now she'd be shunned. It wasn't as though she was a young person going on their *rumspringa* before baptism. Leaving the community after baptism was a serious thing. Mary Lou's mother was staring at him, waiting for him to speak.

"Is there something you want me to do?"

"You could've married her years ago and this wouldn't have happened."

He looked down at the ground. *Her mother is right. You should have thought more deeply about whether Mary Lou was the right one and when you weren't feeling it, you should've let her go.*

"Can you persuade her to come back?"

He looked into Mary Lou's mother's eyes. "I don't even know where she is."

"She still works at the bakery. Can't you go and see her there?"

He nodded. "I'll do that. I'll let you know how it goes."

"Very good." Mrs. White hurried away after giving him another frown.

He knew the chances of her coming back to the community any time soon weren't good. The only thing that Mary Lou was interested in was getting married and he couldn't offer her that now. Not now that he was in love with Hazel.

Against Isaac's better judgment, he waited outside the bakery café for Mary Lou to finish her shift. When she walked out the door, she looked up and saw him right away. Now she was wearing the same uniform as the other non-Amish workers from the bakery—a short pink dress with short sleeves. It saddened him to see that she'd cut her hair, and it now sat on the top of her shoulders. He didn't want to be the cause of anyone falling and now he was.

She walked over to him. "What do you want?"

"I came to talk to you. Your *mudder* told me that you left the community."

"I did. There was nothing there for me anymore, thanks to you." Her words made him feel worse. "Why don't you go off somewhere with Hazel?"

"Hazel has left. Her *mudder* is very ill."

"I'm sorry to hear that. What did you want to talk with me about?"

"I hope you know that when you left, everyone was very upset—naturally."

She looked down at her hand, slowly pressing her fingertips into her palm. "Well, why did you come here?"

"Because I care about you and want the best for you."

"But you don't care about me enough to marry me?"

He looked into her eyes. "I don't love you, Mary Lou. I thought I did once, and I'm sorry I wasted your time."

Tears came into her eyes. "I knew it."

"I still care about you as a dear friend and I don't want me to be the reason you've left the community."

"So, it's about you? You came to see me to absolve your guilt?"

"Nee, not at all. I came here to see you because I care about you and I want you to be in *Gott's haus* for eternity. I don't want you to be a lost soul, and it has nothing to do with me or my guilt. *Gott* has to judge what I've done and I'm prepared to take responsibility and stand in judgment for my sins."

A yellow car pulled up close by and the driver honked the horn.

Mary Lou turned her head. "There's my ride. See you 'round, Isaac."

"Wait!"

She continued to walk away, and then got into the car and it zoomed off. He could only hope that his words might sink into her head and take effect.

Weeks later.

HAZEL'S MOTHER was doing a lot better. Hazel had managed to find a part time cleaning job to bring in some money. It wasn't much, and it all went to keeping herself and her mother in food and helping out with their board at Aunt Bee's house.

The medical bills were mounting and Aunt Bee and

Onkel Luke were doing their best to keep on top of them. The bishop suggested a fundraiser to ease the burden for them.

The fundraising auction was on this coming Saturday. Hazel's mother was embarrassed because the event had been widely publicized and now everyone would know she was ill.

On Friday night, Hazel's mother had gone to bed early and Hazel sat up talking in the living room with Aunt Bee and *Onkel* Luke. Hazel recalled her father always teased Aunt Bee behind her back, calling her 'Can't Be' and calling *Onkel* Luke '*Onkel* Nuke.' Even as a child, she hadn't found his teasing funny. It had been out of malice and not out of affection for her mother's relations.

"Your *mudder* is doing a lot better now," *Onkel* Luke said.

"She is." Hazel knew her mother was only doing better because she was back for good and had told her mother she wouldn't leave her again. "I do hope we raise a lot of money tomorrow to cover all these bills." Hazel was thankful to the community for raising funds. It would take a lot of pressure off their shoulders.

"Trust in *Gott*," *Onkel* Luke said.

Hazel nodded. She did trust in God, but sometimes she couldn't help wondering why God would have chosen to put her mother and herself through all these trials.

Luke and Bee were going through the trials right along with them. Hazel thanked them almost daily, expressing how grateful she was to them. If she was ever in a better position and able to help someone else, she would without hesitating. They had given her a great example.

"I'll say good night. I've got an early start in the morning. I'm off to bed," Uncle Luke said.

"I think I'm too excited to go to sleep," Hazel said. "Or too nervous."

Aunt Bee nodded. "Me too. You go on ahead, Luke. I'll stay up a while and talk with Hazel."

"Very well." Uncle Luke headed up the stairs.

Aunt Bee sighed. "In hindsight, I suppose I shouldn't have told you to stay away when your *mudder* was so fragile."

"You thought you were doing the right thing."

Aunt Bee shook her head. "It's hard to know what to do when you've never been in a situation like this. It's hard to sit by and watch you waste the best years of your life caring about your *mudder* when you should be starting your own life—getting married and having *kinner*."

"There's plenty of time for that. *Mamm's* getting better and better every day."

"Soon, I hope the financial pressure will be off all of us, too."

"That would be nice."

"And then you can concentrate on yourself for a while."

Hazel smiled and wondered what that would be like. She hadn't thought of herself for the longest time. She thought back to the carefree days of the summer vacation when she was a girl and had met Isaac. Why couldn't those carefree days have remained forever? It was a beautiful moment in time before the harsh realities of life had set in.

And what were the chances of meeting Isaac again as an adult? If he hadn't had a girlfriend then things might have been different. Mary Lou seemed to be very much in love with him even though she had slipped. Isaac would've surely forgiven her if she'd repented. Hazel decided she would pray for a man like Isaac. Someone like him would make her feel safe, with his strong body and decisive mind. A man like that would always take care of her.

But not only did she need a man to take care of her, she also needed a man who was willing to take on caring for her mother. She was certain her mother would never be able to live alone. She would always need someone to care for her. Thanks to her father, her mother now had a fear of being left alone.

"I would've thought your *vadder* would've at least tried to contact you. There's been no word from him."

"We're best off not to think about him, Aunt Bee.

And the less *Mamm* thinks of him, the better off she'll be."

"You're right."

"What time do we have to leave here tomorrow morning?" Hazel asked.

"We'll have to leave by eight."

"Okay, I'll wake up at seven."

"Your *mudder* said she's too embarrassed to go."

"I thought you had persuaded her. She should go."

Aunt Bee shook her head. "I did and then she changed her mind back again. Daisy Moulder is coming over to stay with her. She said she'd be here bright and early in the morning."

"Does *Mamm* know about Daisy coming?"

"*Jah*, but I didn't want to give her a chance to talk you into staying too. You have a problem with saying no to your *mudder*."

"It's hard when she's so fragile."

"I know. I learned that the hard way when I asked you to stay away for the weekend that time. I also found out that tough love doesn't work with your *mudder*. She needs to be handled in just the right way."

"*Jah*, very gently."

Aunt Bee nodded again.

CHAPTER 16

News had come to Isaac that there was to be a fundraiser for Hazel's mother. He'd read about it in the Amish newspaper and he'd heard talk of it from two different people. He knew he had to attend. He'd wanted to see Hazel and had also been thinking up a way to help her. A fundraiser was a perfect way to do those two things at once. If he offered Hazel money directly, she'd most likely refuse, but he could do that through the fundraiser with no problem.

He was sitting outside on his parents' porch on that Friday afternoon when Benjamin walked up to him and sat down next to him. "You heard about the fundraiser for Hazel's *mudder?*"

"*Jah,* I've heard."

"Are you going?"

"I've got the bus timetable. I could go and get there in time for it."

Benjamin shook his head. "Just go, Isaac. Don't mess about like you did with Mary Lou. Everyone can tell you're in love with her."

"Hazel?"

"*Jah.*"

"How can everyone tell that?"

"The way you've been in a bad mood ever since she left, for one."

Timothy was walking past just inside the front door and overheard. "He's been in a bad mood all his life," he joked. Timothy stood looking over Benjamin's shoulder, joining in with the conversation.

"*Jah,* but more so after Hazel left," Benjamin said. "Go after her, Isaac."

"I have been thinking about it."

"If she'd ever looked twice at me, I'd go fetch her back. But she's not in love with me."

Isaac looked at Benjamin to see if he was joking. "You think she's in love with me?"

Timothy laughed. "That got your attention, didn't it?"

Isaac rubbed his eyes. "I think I have an auction to go to."

"Can I see you for a minute, Isaac?"

He looked up at the sound of his mother's voice.

"In the kitchen," she added.

He stood and headed toward the kitchen in the midst of hearing his brothers whispering and joking about the fact that he was probably in trouble about something. "What is it, *Mamm?*"

"Have a seat." Once they were seated at the table, she began. "I'm not in the habit of listening in, but I heard what you said just now about going to the fundraiser for Hazel's *mudder.*"

"I think I should go. I want to go. But it will be too hard to see her again." After how he had treated Mary Lou, he felt he didn't deserve any happiness. If Mary Lou returned to the community and married and settled down, then he would be able to pursue his own happiness.

"You're not making any sense."

"It's this way, *Mamm.* I feel dreadful about what I've done to Mary Lou, that I don't deserve happiness when Mary Lou has none. Anyway, who's to say that Hazel likes me? I think she sees me as some kind of tyrant."

"There's one way to find out about Hazel, and you can't be responsible for what happened with Mary Lou."

"You yourself said that I wasted her time."

"I was wrong when I said that to you, Isaac. I was hoping to force you into marrying her because I thought you were just wary of marriage. I didn't know that you were having second thoughts about Mary Lou. That was my mistake. The relationship ending shouldn't have been the cause of her leaving the community. There are always ups and downs in life. That she reacted this way makes me glad you broke things off with her."

"But it was the reason, it was me. You know what the scripture says about standing in someone's way."

"You didn't do it deliberately."

"I might not have done it deliberately, but I caused her great pain and I shouldn't have. I was too caught up in my own selfishness to even think what I was doing to Mary Lou."

"You intended to marry her one day, didn't you?"

"I didn't think things through well enough. I liked spending time with her ... but every time she mentioned marriage, I felt pressured instead of happy."

"You can't hold yourself back thinking about things like that."

His mother was always going to be on his side. She had the mother's ability of seeing the best in him, not seeing his shortcomings the way they really were. "I would like to see Hazel again and tell her how I truly feel about her."

"Ah, I was right." Her eyes sparkled with mischief.

He chuckled. "It's not something that a man generally discusses with his *mudder.*"

"I don't see why not. Everyone needs a little help regarding love sometimes."

"I guess I don't like asking for help."

She chuckled. "You're stubborn just like your *vadder.*"

"Maybe." He looked into his mother's eyes. "Maybe I should take that risk. I'd really love to see her again, and maybe she feels nothing for me, but at least I can go and support the fundraiser."

"That sounds like a good idea."

CHAPTER 17

The very next day, Isaac arrived at the auction site in Allentown, and looked around for Hazel. He couldn't see her anywhere, but he knew he was in the right place and she would be there sometime.

"Isaac Fuller, isn't it?"

Isaac turned around to see a man he'd met recently at a wedding. *"Jah,* it is." Isaac couldn't remember the man's name and was surprised that the fellow had remembered his. He was around the same age, pleasantly plump, with a dark bushy beard.

"It's Albert Troyer."

"Jah, that's right. Sorry, Albert. I remember you, but I just couldn't think of your name. I've had a lot on my mind."

"What brings you to this part of the world?"

"I've come to support the auction, and of course Hazel and her *mudder*. Hazel worked for us briefly."

"I wasn't aware of that."

He nodded. "Before she had to return to look after her *mudder*. Have you seen Hazel around anywhere?"

"Not yet, but I'm sure she's around somewhere. Come and I'll introduce you to some people."

Albert steered him toward a group of men who were looking at farming equipment that was in the line of items to be auctioned.

Hazel traveled with Aunt Bee to the auction. It was hard for her to ask for or to accept help and she felt embarrassed to be placed in that position, but with her *mudder* needing constant attention, *Mamm* had become a full-time job for both Bee and herself.

"Hopefully we'll have a good day today and the money raised will go a long way to helping your mother."

"I hope so."

The women had made food, and the money raised from their stalls and the refreshment stands was also going toward the bills. Hazel was learning the true meaning of family. The community was her family. Her father had failed, but the community had reached out to help and that was something she would never forget.

"I'll let you out here because it looks like I'll have to

park the buggy some distance away. There are a lot of people here."

Hazel looked at the row of buggies. "I'll come with you to park it."

"*Nee* you won't. You get out here. There'll be a lot of people who want to talk to you, and I don't have to be around."

Hazel swallowed her nerves and got out where Aunt Bee suggested she should. She walked toward the table where the auctioneer would stand. A crowd of people had gathered. Then she saw a familiar figure. She was sure it was Isaac. When she got closer, he turned around and she saw that it was he.

"Isaac!"

"Hello."

Her mouth was open and she couldn't speak. Finally, she said, "What are you doing here?"

"I came here for you—to support the auction."

She couldn't believe he was there. His expression was softer, somehow. "Oh, I'm glad you did." After she'd swallowed hard, she asked, "How is everyone?"

"Pretty much the same. Nothing much changes. How's your *mudder* doing?"

"She's so much better now."

"*Gut.*"

"It's nice to see you," she said. He was just as good-looking as she remembered him.

He gave her a big smile. "And you."

She knew her cheeks were red because she could feel them burning. Too embarrassed to look at him, she looked down at her black boots.

"How have you been?"

She glanced back up at him. She was certain they'd exchanged greetings already, but her head was swimming. "I've been good, and you?"

"About the same. We could do with your help back in the office. Things just don't run the same without you. We grew used to having you there."

"I'm glad I was able to help out."

"You did more than that."

A thought occurred to her; he might have come with Mary Lou. "How's Mary Lou?"

"Mary Lou left the community some time ago."

She was stunned at the news and searched his face, wondering if it had something to do with the *Englischer* she'd seen her with. "Really?"

"*Jah,* it's true."

"I hope it wasn't anything to do with me. Maybe I shouldn't have mentioned anything to you."

"We all do what we think is best and that's all we can do. I've come to believe that people are responsible for their own actions and they can't blame other people. I blamed my actions for the longest time in regard to Mary Lou, but I'm through blaming myself."

She had no idea what he meant. Had he meant he blamed himself for Mary Lou leaving the community?

"It's just a surprise, especially seeing you were getting married."

"*Nee*, I never asked her to marry me." He shook his head. "Is that what she said?"

Hazel recalled Mary Lou's words and she was sure Mary Lou had told her they were going to announce their wedding date soon. "I think so. Something like that."

"I think that's where things started to go wrong." He shrugged his shoulders. "I didn't know there was some time limit for dating a girl before you ask her to marry you."

Hazel shook her head. "I wouldn't know anything about that."

"Anyway, I'm not here to talk about Mary Lou, or myself. Today is about you and your *mudder*, and raising a lot of money."

"I hope so. I'm so glad you came. It's so nice to see you. Are you staying with someone?"

"I'm staying at a bed-and-breakfast. I don't really know anyone from this community except a man called Albert Troyer. I met him at a wedding not long ago."

Hazel giggled.

"What's funny?"

"I don't know. Everything and nothing. When this is over, would you come back to Aunt Bee's *haus* where my *mudder* and I are living? She'd loved to meet you. I've told her a lot about you and your family."

"*Jah*, I'd like that very much. *Denke.*"

"Come for the evening meal."

"Are you sure that would be all right with your Aunt Beet?"

She giggled. "It's Aunt Bee."

"Oh." He laughed. "I'm sorry. Aunt Bee."

"You'll come?"

"I'd like nothing more."

"Excuse me, Hazel, can I interrupt for a moment?" They were interrupted by the community's bishop and another man who stood to the side, waiting.

"Oh, Bishop Paul. This is Isaac Fuller. I worked with his family in Lancaster County."

"Hello, Isaac. I know your *vadder* well." They shook hands. "I'm glad you could come here."

"*Denke*, it's *gut* to meet you."

The bishop turned back to Hazel and introduced her to the man who would be auctioneer for the day. Isaac backed away and gave Hazel a little wave. Hazel knew he wouldn't be very far away.

When the auction was about to start, she found Aunt Bee and told her about Isaac having come, and her dinner invitation to him. Then she led Bee to where Isaac was standing, and introduced them to each other.

Soon Hazel stood and watched, with Aunt Bee on

one side of her and Isaac on the other, as the auction started. It embarrassed Hazel when Isaac bid on things she knew he had no use for. Then he donated them back to the auction to be sold again. At the end of the day, the amount Isaac alone had spent came to over five thousand dollars.

"You shouldn't have done that, Isaac," she whispered, feeling both pleased and guilty that he'd given so much money. It was an unbelievably huge sum to her.

"Everyone needs a helping hand every now and again. Who knows? It might be my turn soon." He gave her a beaming smile that melted her insides.

"Are you coming home with us?" Aunt Bee asked Isaac. "We can take you back to the bed-and-breakfast later tonight."

"If that's not going to be too much trouble. I don't want to be under your feet."

"Nonsense. We're pleased to have you join us for dinner."

During the buggy ride back to Bee's house, Isaac said, "It'll be a while before they tally up the amounts raised today, but I'd say they raised a good sum."

"I know. That's so good," Hazel said. *"Denke,* Isaac, for everything you've done."

"It was my pleasure. I've been looking forward to seeing you, so I can talk you into coming back to work for us."

"I don't think my *mudder's* ready for me to leave her again. She might never be ready."

"Bring her with you. Problem solved," he said.

"She's got her doctors and everything here, though. She's not good with change anymore."

When they pulled up at the house, Isaac tried to help Bee with the horse, but she insisted that he go on ahead into the house with Hazel.

"Hazel, I jumped at the chance of coming to the auction because I had to see you again."

She stopped walking and looked up into his eyes. "Did you?"

"*Jah.*"

Excitement rippled through her body, but then she remembered her mother. She took off, walking at a brisk pace. "I must get inside to see my *mudder*."

He ran after her. "Wait, Hazel. I want to talk to you in private."

She stopped again.

"Look into my eyes."

She didn't want to. She didn't want him to offer her happiness because she knew she would have to deny it. Every time she looked at her mother's sad face she didn't want to remember that she had a chance at happiness.

"Hazel, look at me."

Slowly, she looked into his blue eyes.

"Things never worked out with Mary Lou and me because—"

"*Nee*, don't say anything else. Please."

She walked to the door and opened it, and then she turned around and stopped in the doorway. It would be hard for him to talk privately knowing her mother was just inside the house. "Come inside, Isaac, and meet my *mudder*."

At that moment, Isaac figured that Hazel probably didn't feel the same. She had just saved him from an embarrassing moment. Why was life so complicated? Why couldn't Hazel have been devoted to him like Mary Lou had been? Perhaps she had a man. He thought back to those letters he'd seen on the desk, the ones that she'd tried to cover up.

CHAPTER 18

Isaac stepped onto Aunt Bee's porch, took off his hat, and walked inside. Hazel pointed him toward a living room where a small woman sat with her knees covered by a knitted blanket of many colors.

"*Mamm,* this is Isaac Fuller. Remember I told you about all the Fuller boys and working for Mr. Fuller at the kitchen cabinetry place?"

"*Jah,* that's right, when you left me." She looked over at Isaac and smiled. "*Denke* for giving my *dochder* a job."

"I'm pleased to meet you, Mrs. Bauer."

Mrs. Bauer visibly cringed when he said her name. He figured it had something to do with her husband leaving her and still having to be called by his name.

"And it's nice to meet you. Please, call me Judy." She turned to her daughter. "How did the auction go?"

"There was a huge crowd there." Hazel looked over at Isaac as she sat down beside her *mudder*. "Please take a seat."

He sat opposite the two women on the other couch. Mrs. Bauer looked similar to Hazel, only much older, so much so that she looked more like Hazel's grandmother than her mother.

"Isaac bought a lot at the auction."

Isaac was embarrassed that Hazel had mention such a thing. "It was nothing, Hazel."

"Denke, Isaac. We appreciate all your help. I've been a burden on my Hazel for a long time."

"You're not a burden," Hazel insisted a little too loudly.

"I've just caused a lot of people problems."

Hazel patted her mother's hand. "Isaac's staying for dinner. He's staying at a bed-and-breakfast place close by."

"You could've stayed here, Isaac," Mrs. Bauer said.

"Nee, I wouldn't want to put anybody out."

"When do you leave?" Mrs. Bauer asked.

"I'm leaving tomorrow afternoon on the two o'clock bus."

It saddened Hazel to hear that he was leaving. Of course, she already knew it, but now there was no pretending he could stay. She'd have to make the most of having him there. "You'll be at the meeting tomorrow then?" Hazel asked.

"*Jah*, and I've heard that the meeting is being held at the bishop's *haus?*"

Bee walked into the house at that moment. "That's right. Can we collect you from the bed-and-breakfast?"

"That would be *wunderbaar* if you could."

"*Jah*, we can do that."

When they heard a horse and buggy, Bee looked out the open doorway behind her. "That's Luke now." She turned back to face them. "Hazel, why don't you take Isaac outside to meet your *Onkel* Luke?"

"Sure."

When they got outside, Luke had taken the buggy and his horse around the other side of the barn where the stables were.

"I'm sorry if I said something to upset you before, Hazel."

"*Nee*, you didn't upset me. It's just that things are complicated right now."

"I can see that. I can see what kind of situation you're in. It can't be easy for you to feel stuck."

"That's exactly how I feel, and I sometimes feel torn. I want to have my own life and spread my wings, but I can't because my mother needs me. I hope you understand."

"I do, as much as I can without being in the situation myself. I'm glad I came here."

"I am too. It's so good to see you."

He wanted to say more, but a man was walking toward them.

"Here's *Onkel* Luke now." Hazel introduced Luke and Isaac, and then they all went into the house.

HAZEL WANTED to tell Isaac that she liked him too. She'd wait for another opportunity so she could let him know. If he was prepared to wait, then something good might finally come her way.

They sat in the living room sipping hot chocolate that Aunt Bee had prepared for them. It was just the thing for a late autumn afternoon. Aunt Bee's hot chocolate was like no one else's. They were drinking silken-smooth chocolate. Hazel had watched how her aunt made it, but hadn't had the chance to make it by herself.

While Isaac complimented Bee on the unique taste of the hot chocolate, Hazel watched him. His deep blue eyes were filled with kindness along with compassion.

"How did that audit problem go?" Hazel asked Isaac.

"We had to pay another five hundred dollars and that was it. We got no fine."

"*Ah, gut.*"

"*Dat* said to thank you for sorting things out for us."

"It sounds like you did a good job for the Fuller family," Hazel's mother said.

"She did. She fitted in so well."

Hazel giggled and when everyone looked at her, she told them how awkward things were when Isaac first saw her sitting in his chair.

Isaac laughed along with her, and explained to the others, "You see, my *vadder* didn't tell me he'd employed anyone. I walked in thinking we'd been robbed and I'd be faced with a masked robber wielding a weapon, and then I saw Hazel in my office sitting at my desk tapping away at my computer. *Dat* had given her my office."

"She was almost a thief; she'd stolen your office," Luke said, which made everyone laugh.

"*Jah*, she stole my office and then she stole all of our hearts," Isaac said.

Hazel giggled. "I don't know about that."

Luke said, "It's not easy working in a family business."

"Luke was working in his family's business when we met," Bee said.

"*Jah*, but I didn't stay in it for long." He turned to Isaac. "Maybe you won't be there for long either."

That hadn't even occurred to Hazel. Maybe Isaac might leave and move closer.

"*Nee*, I wouldn't know what else to do. You see, I have six brothers and the business is their livelihood and it's always been my *vadder's* plan, and mine, that it would support our future families as well."

"It must be a big business to do that," Bee said.

"It's growing," Isaac said. *"Denke* to *Gott."*

THAT NIGHT, Luke, along with Hazel, drove Isaac back to his bed-and-breakfast. When Hazel got home, she peeped into her mother's bedroom and saw her sleeping soundly. Then she tiptoed into her bedroom, which was right next door.

When Hazel slipped between the sheets, she closed her eyes and thanked God for the day. They might have raised enough to pay all the bills, and Isaac had come to see her.

Could she and Isaac have a proper relationship? She was certain he liked her and 'felt that way' about her. Since he hadn't seemed to be in a hurry to marry Mary Lou, maybe he wouldn't mind waiting for her, but how long would he have to wait? She didn't see that her mother would ever leave the town she felt comfortable in, and Isaac would never move there; he'd as good as said so. The next time he tried to say anything to her, she'd listen to what he had to say.

WHEN ISAAC GOT BACK to the bed-and-breakfast, he realized he didn't want to go back home without telling Hazel how he felt about her. He'd tried once, but she had deliberately interrupted him. He took his hat off and placed it on the bed and then undid the top button of his shirt. His mind traveled back to those letters Hazel had tried to hide. Did she have another man? There had been no one else by her side today, so he figured she couldn't have had another man who was very significant in her life. And if she did, he would convince her that he was the best man for her.

HAZEL KNEW she would never have to worry about anything ever again with a solid man such as Isaac. He was devoted to his family and wasn't the kind of man who would run away after another woman. He was the opposite of how her father had been. But then there was her mother to consider. Even though her mother was better now, Hazel was sure she wouldn't consider moving to Lancaster County. She closed her eyes tightly and prayed for God to work everything out.

If she had faith, God would make a way for them. She recalled from the Scriptures that if one had faith as small as a mustard seed, then mountains would be moved. Hazel needed a mountain to be moved.

The next morning, Hazel was up early. She was in the utility room pressing her Sunday-best dress so she would look as good as she possibly could.

Then she heard her mother calling her. She set the iron back on the holder and hurried up the stairs, hoping that her mother hadn't woken Bee and Luke. It was still early and she knew they'd been tired after the auction.

When she opened her mother's door, she saw her sitting up in bed. "What is it, *Mamm?*"

Her mother coughed. "I don't think I'm well enough to go to the meeting today."

She moved closer and sat on her mother's bed. "Are you sick?" She leaned forward and pressed the back of her hand to her mother's forehead. "You don't feel hot."

"I think I have the flu coming on."

"That's no good. Can I bring some breakfast up to you?"

"I don't feel like anything. Perhaps just a hot cup of tea?"

"Of course." Hazel hurried back to the kitchen and filled up the kettle and placed it on the stove. Then she finished ironing her dress. She didn't exactly resent her mother, but sometimes she felt more like she was the mother, and her mother was the child. A pang of bitterness ran through her heart. Her mother was standing in the way of her happiness. It didn't seem fair. Then she reminded herself of the prayer that she had prayed just as she'd been drifting off to sleep. She had to trust *Gott* that everything would work out. Or did He expect her to come up with a plan? She shook her head. He wouldn't do that because she would never be able to come up with a plan.

When she had made her mother a cup of tea, she

carefully draped her newly ironed dress over her arm and headed up the stairs to her mother.

"There you are, *Mamm.*"

"*Denke.* Sit down and talk to me for a moment. Do you have the time?"

"I do. I got up early to iron my dress." She draped her dress over one side of the bed and then sat down by her mother.

"I can tell Isaac likes you very much."

"I like him too."

"Just make sure he is not a man like your *vadder.*"

"*Nee,* he's not. I just know he's not."

"I hope you're right. I wouldn't want to see you have a broken heart like my heart was broken. I wouldn't say that all men are bad, because I know they're not. Sometimes it's hard, though, to tell the good from the bad—to separate the wheat from the chaff."

"I put everything in *Gott's* hands, *Mamm.*"

"You'll never leave me, will you?"

"Of course I won't."

Her mother smiled. "It will always be you and me together, won't it?" She reached for Hazel's hand and Hazel took her hand and put her other hand on top.

"*Jah,* it will always be us. Together forever."

"You won't be going back to Lancaster County, will you?"

"Not that I know of."

"Good."

"Now drink your tea, *Mamm*, before it goes cold." She got up, leaned over, and kissed her mother on the forehead. "I'll say goodbye before we head off to the meeting." She carefully picked up her dress and walked into her bedroom, feeling low. For a moment there she had thought her mother was going to say that if she found a man she loved to hang on to him and not let him go.

Isaac paced back and forth in his small room. It was adequate, but the room's decor was totally suited to a woman with its bright pink swagged curtains and the lacy bedspread. He chuckled quietly.

Finally, a knock sounded on his door. His breakfast was arriving and it was ten minutes late. He didn't want to be late when Hazel's Uncle Luke came to collect him for the early-morning Sunday meeting.

"Good morning," the old woman crowed.

"Morning," Isaac said.

"You'll be leaving today then?"

"I will. I'll take everything with me when I leave in half an hour."

"I hope you enjoyed your stay."

He looked down at his bacon and eggs and coffee, which were growing cold. "I did. Now I'll enjoy this breakfast."

She smiled at him and stepped back.

After he had closed the door, he carefully placed the tray on the small table. Normally bacon and eggs was what he preferred for breakfast but this morning he was sick to his stomach thinking this might be the last time he saw Hazel for some time. It didn't sit right with him. He had to make one last effort to win her over and have her come back to Lancaster County with him.

HAZEL PULLED HER DRESS ON, trying her best not to resent her mother. *Mamm* couldn't help being clingy with her fragile mental state. She was so happy that Isaac had come to see her that she didn't want to think about how low she'd feel when he left. Then she reminded herself that she couldn't let a man determine her mood or she'd end up like her mother. She had to be happy no matter what.

It wasn't long before Hazel was traveling in the buggy with her Uncle Luke and Aunt Bee, on the way to collect Isaac for the meeting. When they came close to the bed-and-breakfast, she could see him standing outside waiting for them. He looked so handsome in his black suit and hat, standing so tall and straight.

She carefully adjusted her prayer *kapp* and hoped that he would find her appearance pleasing.

He greeted her aunt and uncle and then climbed into the back seat with her.

"Hello, Hazel." He had a small bag with him that he

put by his feet. It was a reminder that he was soon going to be leaving.

"Hello." She could tell by the way he looked at her that he was in love with her. She was certain of it.

Then her uncle started chatting with him and she knew they wouldn't be able to have any private words until the meal was served, after the meeting was over.

HAZEL WAS RUNNING out of time. Soon her uncle would be driving Isaac to the bus stop and Isaac had a crowd gathered around him.

"Who's your friend?"

She looked over to see a good friend of hers, Becky. Becky was nearly six feet tall and, she joked, just as wide. Everyone loved Becky for her jolly personality. "Hi, Becky. I worked for Isaac. Remember I told you about Isaac and his family?"

"*Jah.* I saw him at the auction yesterday. I was there briefly before I had to leave for work. Why are you looking so stressed?"

She glanced over at Isaac. "It's just that he's leaving soon and I want to talk to him. I don't have a chance with everyone around."

Becky looked over at Isaac. "Some of those people are leaving now. Leave it to me."

Before Hazel could say anything, Becky marched over and said something to the crowd and marched back holding onto Isaac's arm. Hazel was embarrassed, wondering what Becky had said. But no one was looking at her except for Isaac who had his eyes fixed onto hers.

"Here he is," Becky said with a quick little grin before she walked away.

"What did she say to you?" Hazel asked.

"She said there was someone I needed to speak with."

"Oh, that's embarrassing."

"*Nee* it's not. Come, let's walk this way so we can speak privately."

They headed to a quiet corner of the bishop's yard. "I wanted to speak to you before you left."

"*Jah?*"

She nodded.

"What did you want to say?"

"I don't know. Nothing I haven't said before. Things would be different if I didn't have to look after my *mudder*. I guess I just wanted you to know that."

"And if she wasn't a problem you'd come back with me?"

"*Jah.*"

"You mean it? You'd marry me?"

Hazel gasped. "Marry?"

"*Jah.* What were you talking about?"

"Oh, I'm not certain."

"Marry me, and we can have a cat or two." He smiled at her.

"Oh, maybe we should get to know one another better and see … Marriage sounds good to me." She had to be totally honest and let him know how she felt. She might not get another chance.

"So, if it's all right with your *mudder,* you'll move to Lancaster County and marry me?"

She giggled. "It sounds like a dream." Then she got serious. "You know how fragile my *mudder* is."

"She can come with us and live with us. My *haus* is plenty big enough."

This was something she'd already thought through. "All her doctors are around here."

"She'll have to change doctors. There are many fine doctors in Lancaster County. We'll find her the best ones." He looked around.

"What are you looking for?"

"Your *onkel* and aunt. I need to make a detour before Luke takes me to the bus stop." He hurried away and left her standing there.

She stood and watched him talk to her *onkel* and aunt and then after a few words, Bee and Isaac hurried toward the buggy. Not wanting to worry her mother, she tried to stop them, but *Onkel* Luke caught up with her.

"Let them go, Hazel."

She swung around to face Luke. "She's not strong enough."

"Too bad!"

Hazel's jaw dropped.

"You've never had time to be a child or a teenager. It might not be her fault, but she can start putting you first. That man is willing to marry you, and he wants to make it known to your mother, and ask if she'll live with the both of you. He's a very good man, to make that offer to her."

Hazel wanted to be there when her mother made that big decision. "I don't want her to think that everyone is making decisions for her."

"You're talking as though moving to Lancaster County and living with you will be a bad thing for the both of you."

Hazel slowly nodded. "It'll be the best thing. I only hope she can see that."

Luke nodded. "She'll see sense."

"I hope so. I only hope she doesn't tell Isaac yes and then go back on it later."

"We won't let her."

Hazel silently sent up another prayer. Her entire future depended on what happened in the next half hour.

"She's a tricky one. I mean, she's genuinely ill, but I

think she plays on it a bit for sympathy. I don't think she wants a man to come between herself and Hazel."

Isaac regarded Bee's words carefully as they drove the short distance to her house to talk to Hazel's mother. "I hope she'll see I'm serious about Hazel."

"You'll have to do your best to convince her."

"I will. *Denke* for driving me here. How long have I got?"

"You've got fifteen minutes to convince her, if you want to make that bus."

"Okay."

"And we'll still have enough time to go back to the bishop's *haus* to collect Luke and Hazel."

When they got to Bee's house, they found Hazel's mother sitting on the couch.

Isaac took a deep breath and set a smile on his face. He felt better knowing that Bee was going to help him.

Judy looked up at them as if she knew something was going on. "What is it?"

As the two of them sat on a couch opposite, Bee said, "Isaac has something to say."

He opened his mouth and let the words come out without trying to think too much about them. "I'm in love with your *dochder* and she's in love with me. She won't leave here and come back with me, or even continue a relationship with me because she's concerned about you."

"It's her choice. I've got nothing to do with it. She's a grown woman."

Bee said, "So, you're fine if she moves away and lives in Lancaster County again?"

"I'd miss her of course, but if that's what she wants to do, she should do it."

Isaac wasn't entirely convinced she'd say the same thing to Hazel. "Would you come with us and live with us after we're married?"

"Married?" Her bottom lip quivered and she coughed as though trying to cover what she was truly feeling. "That's a big step."

"Not really. Not when two people are in love."

She raised her eyebrows on hearing the L word.

Bee said, "This is going to happen, Judy, so decide what you want to do. Either stay with Luke and me or live with Isaac and Hazel. They're in love and—"

"Why isn't Hazel here for this discussion?"

Isaac shot Bee a look of desperation.

Bee licked her lips. "She's too scared of upsetting you."

Judy turned to Isaac and asked him, "She wants to marry you?"

"*Jah*, she said so. She's hesitating because she's worried about you."

"And you'll be good to her?"

He chuckled. "I'll treat her like the special woman she is. I've never been in love like this. You see, I met her in Falls Creek when I was twelve or thirteen while I was on vacation with my family."

"You did? She never mentioned it. Bee lived at Falls Creek."

He nodded. "Hazel told me she must've been there staying at Bee's. I was so taken with her that I was silly enough to propose back then. I was a mere child, couldn't have been any more than thirteen, or maybe even twelve, but I never forgot those eyes. Those beautiful eyes."

"She does have lovely eyes."

"I nearly married someone else, I got to the verge of thinking I should propose, but I wanted to capture that connection, that feeling, that I had once found with that wonderful green-eyed girl I'd met at Falls Creek. You see, I never thought I'd see her again. When I walked in and saw her that first day at the workshop, I was shocked as I recalled her face. Then, I was sure she wasn't the one because when I met her, she'd gone by the name of Livy."

"*Jah,* her first name is Olivia, but she never liked it so she started having everyone call her Hazel, which is her middle name."

"Ah, I wondered where the name 'Livy' came from."

"I am happy for you to marry Hazel."

"You are?" He could scarcely believe his ears.

"*Jah,* I believe you are a genuine person if you've thought about her for that long."

"I did. She was never far from my mind even though I didn't know her. There was something about her."

Bee put a gentle hand on his shoulder as if to tell him not to oversell now that he had her approval. "You've got that bus to catch, Isaac. We'll collect Hazel and Luke on our way and tell them the good news."

He leaped to his feet and held his hand out to Hazel's mother. She smiled and grabbed his hand as tears welled in her eyes. "Look after her."

"I will. I will put her first in everything. And you are very welcome to live with us. I have a large *haus.*"

"*Denke.* I will give it some thought."

"We better go, Isaac," Bee said.

They hurried out of the house.

When Hazel saw Isaac hurrying toward her, she knew from his beaming face that it was good news.

He reached her and said, "She's given us her blessing. We can marry."

"What?" Hazel was now worried her mother would go back on it.

"Bee was there and heard it all. We have to go now for the bus, but I'll call you tomorrow and we'll start making arrangements for the wedding. I want to marry you as soon as possible." The words had slipped out of his mouth and they almost shocked him. Now he wasn't afraid, or unprepared for marriage. He wanted to be married, but only to Hazel. No longer did he want to enjoy his own company for an extended period of time. He wanted to be with the woman he loved.

"I can scarcely believe it."

"Am I moving too quickly?"

"Nee, not at all. This is *wunderbaar.* What did my mother say?"

"I'll tell you on the way to the bus station. Bee is waiting in the buggy and we have to find Luke."

WHEN HAZEL GOT home after they'd taken Isaac to the bus station, she was prepared for her mother to say she had second thoughts about her marrying. She found her mother lying in bed.

"How are you feeling, *Mamm?"* She sat on the edge of her bed.

"Excited for you and Isaac."

"Really?"

"I like him a lot."

Hazel heaved a sigh of relief.

"He told me how he feels about you."

"Will you come to live with us?"

"I think that would make sense, if you don't mind having me there. I don't want to be under your feet when you're newly married. Perhaps I'll stay here for a time and then live with you and Isaac?"

Hazel could scarcely believe it. Tears came to her eyes. "He said we could have a cat, or even two. I never was allowed to have one."

"Ah, a cat. There's nothing like animals to make a house into a home, and of course, *kinner*."

"I hope we'll have plenty of them."

"*Gott* has blessed you with a *gut mann*. There's no reason you won't have many *kinner*."

THE NEXT MORNING, Hazel stayed by the phone in the barn and waited for Isaac's call. It felt as though she was living someone else's life. It had been so long since anything good had come her way. When the phone rang, she picked it up after one ring. "Hello?"

"It's me."

"Hi."

"How's your *mudder* today?"

"Still going along with the plan."

"And you?"

"I'm fine."

"And are you still on-board with the plan?"

She giggled. "Of course I am."

"Good. I've already spoken to the bishop and we can have our wedding in six weeks here in Lancaster. You and your *mudder* can stay at my parents' *haus*, a day, a week, or however long you need to before the wedding."

"That soon?"

"*Jah.* I told you I want to marry you as soon as I can. I love you, Hazel."

Those were the words she'd longed to hear. "And I love you."

"*Gott* brought us together."

"I know."

"I'm going to build onto my *haus* so your *mudder* can have a separate space."

"For real?"

"*Jah.* It'll be done by the time we're married."

"That's *wunderbaar*. She'll be so happy."

Isaac loved to hear Hazel's voice and couldn't wait to see her again. He'd have to organize another visit before their wedding. "Now I'll have to tell my folks about us getting married. They'll be excited. So will my brothers."

"I hope so."

"They will. My *mudder* really likes you. So does *Dat*, and you know Benjamin does."

Hazel giggled and it filled Isaac's heart with joy as he imagined her laughter ringing through their home and bringing peace and comfort. "I know your life hasn't been easy, Hazel, but that stops today. I'll do everything I can, and with *Gott's* help, you'll have a good life with me."

"I know it, Isaac, I just know it."

At the same time, Isaac and Hazel sent up silent prayers of thanks to God for finding them each their perfect partner.

> *God is not a man, that he should lie;*
> *neither the son of man, that he should repent:*
> *hath he said, and shall he not do it?*
> *or hath he spoken, and shall he not make it good?*
> Numbers 23:19

~

Thank you for reading The Amish Bachelor,

Book #1 *Seven Amish Bachelors.* I hope you enjoyed it.

Blessings,

Samantha Price

SEVEN AMISH BACHELORS

SEVEN AMISH BACHELORS series:
Book 1 The Amish Bachelor
Book 2 His Amish Romance
Book 3 Joshua's Choice
Book 4 Forbidden Amish Romance
Book 5 The Quiet Amish Bachelor
Book 6 The Determined Amish Bachelor
Book 7 Amish Bachelor's Secret

ABOUT SAMANTHA PRICE

USA Today Bestselling author, Samantha Price, wrote stories from a young age, but it wasn't until later in life that she took up writing full time. Formally an artist, she exchanged her paintbrush for the computer and, many best-selling book series later, has never looked back.

Samantha is happiest on her computer lost in the world of her characters. She is best known for the Ettie Smith Amish Mysteries series and the Expectant Amish Widows series.

www.SamanthaPriceAuthor.com

Samantha loves to hear from her readers. Connect with her at:

samantha@samanthapriceauthor.com
www.facebook.com/SamanthaPriceAuthor
Follow Samantha Price on BookBub
Twitter @ AmishRomance
Instagram - SamanthaPriceAuthor

Made in the USA
Monee, IL
21 November 2021